# CONTENTS

Raef Boylan, *Nights Out*   9
Ralph Bullivant, *The Taste of Burnt Mackerel*   15
Max Dunbar, *The Shot*   22
Rory Gleeson, *Dart Times*   27
Anthony Howcroft, *Killer*   35
David Martin, *Relic*   44
Duncan Ross, *Stillness*   49
Fee Simpson, *Derek and his Clown*   55
Rebecca Swirsky, *On the Origin of the Species*   59
Barney Walsh, *Somebody Else's Lie*   66

# Introduction

2013 is the first year that The Big Issue in the North has run the New Writing Award. Our aim in establishing the award was to raise funds for The Big Issue in the North Trust, the charity arm of the magazine, whilst also supporting new writers and their careers. Teaming up with Valley Press, Creative Industries Trafford, Waterside Arts Centre and Manchester Literature Festival, we were able to raise a prize of £1000 for first place. This anthology contains the ten short stories that were shortlisted for the award.

The Big Issue in the North Trust supports some of the most vulnerable people in our communities, striving to improve the lives of people who are homeless or vulnerably housed, and those who find it difficult to enter the mainstream jobs market. It was for those people that this award was launched and it is because of them that we wish to continue it in the years to come.

Fifty per cent of the revenue from sales of this book will go to funding the Trust to continue this work. During the period that the award was active, we also worked with a number of creative writing tutors who came into our centres to help our service users engage with creative writing as a means of expression – helping to break isolation.

In the end it was Anthony Howcroft's 'Killer' that received the award. A suspenseful and tense exploration of the nature of guilt, Howcroft's story was chosen because of the simple but effective storytelling that it used to build to its sinister conclusion.

This year's judges were Jamie McGarry, editor of Valley Press, Kevin Gopal, editor of The Big Issue in the North, and David Gaffney, acclaimed short story writer. Picking one winner from well over a hundred submissions was difficult, but the judges felt that the shortlist of ten stories they arrived at served to illustrate the talent in contemporary British short literature.

We hope that you enjoy this anthology and continue to support The Big Issue in the North, independent publishers and new writers.

The Big Issue in the North would like to thank Valley Press, Creative Industries Trafford, Waterside Arts Centre, Manchester Literature Festival, the International Anthony Burgess Foundation, Jamie McGarry, Kevin Gopal and David Gaffney.

*Nathan Connolly*
*Project Coordinator, The New Writing Award*
*The Big Issue in the North*
*www.bigissueinthenorth.com*

# NIGHTS OUT

*Raef Boylan*

The boy had never felt so alone. Sometimes the sky felt so high it was beyond reach but now its black mass was oppressively close, overwhelming and almost suffocating. He splayed his hand out an inch from his face and could barely distinguish it from the night. This made him laugh a little, nervously. What if the sky should swallow him? Who could stop it? There were a few stars, blinking. Or maybe they were aeroplanes, en route to Majorca. The boy wished they were going somewhere more exotic, like Russia or India, but Majorca was more likely. He knew his city, had lived here for the whole seventeen years of his existence. Seventeen wasn't very old; in terms of the planet's historical tapestry he was a mere speck. Insignificant. That was the right word to describe how the sky made him feel too: insignificant. He mouthed it silently. The five syllables appeared sharp and angry. Or was it just that *he* was angry? Why would he be angry – it hadn't been such a bad day?

One of the stars had vanished. He figured that meant it had been a plane. Unless he'd just witnessed its final dying gasps. Only, hadn't they been taught that some stars were so far away, by the time the light reached Earth you might be looking at ones that had already burned out? Either way: death throes. It bothered him; he tried to spot the aeroplane by tracing each of its possible journeys, but could find no moving objects. Perhaps the sky had swallowed the plane. Pretty different destination to Majorca, he reckoned. That was funny, in a sick way. Was he sick? He focused on the panic and screams as the metal bird twisted and disintegrated; a mother shoving the oxygen mask over her toddler's face; the kid choking on its own terrified snot, uncomprehending. This vision, the human details, made him wince and shove-eject it from his brain. No, he wasn't sick.

Remembering the bottle planted between his feet, the boy retrieved it and took a jerky swig. Some liquid spilled down his chin and he wiped it off with his bare arm. Would a serial killer get off on the thought of planes being ripped apart mid-air? Maybe the lack of control would be too disturbing. He wondered, not for the first time, how it felt to kill someone, to look down on a body stilled forever by your own desire. How could you not crack up, feeling the heavy cloud of your deeds hovering over every sandwich you ate, every time you took a dump? Were all serial killers devoid of conscience or was the adrenaline rush instantly addictive, too good to give up? Fuck, where was the line? He knew he'd killed ants, must have done simply by walking around. Plus he'd deliberately killed a few wasps and spiders in his time. Thwack. Was that murder? Fishermen and people working in abattoirs didn't necessarily progress to killing people, and presumably slept OK at night. So did the line begin with your own species? Or was it all about method and deliberation? Luring a neighbour's cat into your microwave probably signalled crossing the line.

Could you kill a cat and walk away from the whole business, like someone who tries heroin once and never spirals into addiction? Or would the taste be too much and drive you to kill another cat and another and another – until cats aren't enough and then dogs aren't enough and then you're walking down the street sizing up every fellow human being like potential prey? He wondered how close the nearest murderer lived. A few miles? A few streets? Next-door to his parents? If he found out his dad had killed someone, what would he do: grass him up, leg it or just carry on as normal? No. How could anything be normal when you knew that? Did serial killers ever get out of prison and go back to their wives or mothers? Holy crap, imagine trying to sleep at night. Locks on the inside of your door... or maybe on the outside of theirs. *Welcome back from prison, now please go to your room and stay there.* Pretty messed up. Would it be worse to be murdered than just dying naturally? Depended on where your fear of death derived from, he guessed. With some people it was what happened to the body afterwards, of becoming an object. To be burnt by a vicar or to be buried beneath a killer's patio, that was the question.

It all stank of indignity. The boy wanted a cigarette now, always did when meditating on mortality. He fished the packet out of his jeans, counted the filters by touch and discovered he hadn't enough to last until morning, unless he slowed right down. He'd been smoking too much lately, since school broke up for summer. Regular wage was going to kill him. Pretty ironic, considering all the shouting his dad used to do about him not having a job. He lit up and inhaled through the web of phlegm at the back of his throat. Didn't sound pretty. Neither did cancer. But what else to do with your hands? A starlit wank might be kind of cool, a pure Jim Carroll moment – but not right now. Some night he'd come back to this field, and try not to reflect on serial killers.

The smoke was harsh so he washed the taste away with a few more swigs from his bottle; a wet throat always helped. Somebody was tapping on his shoulder, calling his name. Reluctantly he turned to face them. *You alright, Simon? You zoned out for a minute there.* She wanted him to come back down to earth, back to the party. The others wanted him to come back. Someone's iPod speakers were blaring out the latest pseudo-rock anthem. Somebody else couldn't find the bottle-opener, and was told to use their girlfriend's teeth. Another someone said Jonesy had been sick. He drained his bottle and reached into the stash of carrier bags for another. The elusive bottle-opener made the rounds into his hand and he prised the drink open with teenage expertise. Other people had cigarettes, he'd be fine. He tried to tune into the conversation. *Emma and Wayne, I saw them getting in the taxi together... there's no more Stella, you'll have to move onto Fosters... I'll do you a copy of the album if you want... so, what, are they going out now or... who drank my Stella then?... there's schnapps as well somewhere... is it worth trying to get tickets... yeah, yeah, they're good live...* He felt guilty that none of it struck him as interesting, like a gatecrasher trying unsuccessfully to fit in.

These were his friends, then? Their faces, in the faint glow of mobile phones and a camping lantern, were contorted and alien. He took violent drags on the cigarette like he was playing a part in some moody art film, and waited to be yanked into talk. At some point there'd be an argument, over a misunderstanding or someone's drunken insensitivity; the offended party would storm home, followed by laments and a sympathetic chaperone. One of the girls would need the toilet and refuse to try peeing al fresco; no one would offer a solution so she'd also go home and possibly not return. They'd run out of drink; someone's dad would have more in his garage and there would be an attempted raid. Nick Jones would be sick again. Lisa would probably be sick too, make herself purge the calorific alcopops she'd consumed and then start crying. Alternatively, she'd wander off without telling anyone and there would be a half-hour of panicky texts and phone-calls – whichever Lisa deemed would achieve the most attention.

How to help Lisa? It was becoming apparent that no one could. Pretty soon she'd wind up in hospital again for a few months, where they'd force her back onto a drip and watch her going to the toilet. That had to suck. Gradually getting less invitations to these kind of parties because people just couldn't handle the stress of making sure she didn't hurt herself. She'd begged him to bring a piece of glass to the clinic; sitting on that sterile-white bed, scarred appendages wrapped around her bony knees – *Please, Si.* He could have done it, but what if she'd used the glass to kill herself? Same deal as being a murderer: you couldn't escape knowledge of responsibility. Something suddenly stroked his knee. The hand grasping his fresh bottle jerked, spilling drops of lager on the grass and his trainers. Jade. What did she want? He hadn't even noticed her sidle up to him, scooting purposefully across the ground on her bum. She took possession of his other hand and draped it over her leg – and he was passive as a mannequin, just allowed her to do it.

Jade was Lauren's best friend. Lauren was in Cyprus. Lauren had almost been his girlfriend. Three weeks of coming over to his house to watch TV like nobody else owned a TV, sitting practically on his lap, asking did he fancy this girl or that girl. Fooling around. Play-fights. He'd paid for her Meatball Sub. Then Thursday, the day before she left the country. He wondered what Lauren had divulged to Jade about Thursday. It's not like he hadn't suspected; he'd put clean sheets on the bed, worn new boxers, showered. He wouldn't get off on a defence plea of naivety. Turned out, he wouldn't get off full stop. Wished they'd tried it at her house instead. He still had to sleep in that bed; the whole thing – mattress, pillows, duvet – reeked of humiliation. Lying awake, thinking of a bikini-clad

Lauren smiling at sculpted Cypriot waiters; they would feed her olives and convince her to take romantic walks along the shore. How could he not be ready at seventeen? Attractive girl tugging at his belt and he felt nothing but empty, cold, a little repulsed. Why did she have to ruin everything? They'd been having a good time.

He wasn't gay. Lauren asked if he was gay and he called her egocentric. She was pretty but so what? Didn't make her the epitome of sexual desire, didn't make him gay that he wanted to spend time together and attempt philosophical debates and maybe kiss her but not – not that. Not stick anything inside her just because biological design dictated that it should be so. Time was ticking. Waste of an empty house, waste of his youth. He stalled. Went to the toilet, chastised his dick – *what's the matter with you?* Brought back two glasses, more whisky than coke; she didn't like the taste, he drank them both. Didn't mean to insult her by needing chemical assistance but she was NAKED under the sheets; not his fault that she couldn't take a hint, couldn't sense his reluctance as he stripped under her instruction and closed the curtains so it was less bright. Clutching the little square packet, but she took it from him, started guiding his fingers under the sheets, whispering encouragement. He felt like a stupid kid. The girl was supposed to be scared and the man was supposed to take charge, but he was no man, that much was clear now. Brushed up against the labial goal posts, a crude playground litany cycling round his brain: pussy... cunt... twat... minge... Pulled away. There was too much flesh for one bed, it felt creepy. Lauren didn't get it. Sniffling, she gave up, put on her clothes and left.

He didn't even see her to the door; too stunned. Cried a little after she'd gone. Life was suddenly a lot less simple. He felt excluded from something that others could take for granted – that HE'D taken for granted half an hour ago. Now it transpired he was a sexual freak, and even though that sounded like it could be a Red Hot Chilli Peppers track, it sure as shit didn't make him feel like dancing. More like blowing his brains out. And now Jade, kneading his hand like squidgy human dough, resting her head on his shoulder and laughing softly – *God, I'm so drunk.* So what, he thought, does that automatically erase loyalty to your best friend? Or was this some kind of signal, Lauren telling him via Jade that they were over?

'Over': his turn to laugh softly, at the soap-opera melodrama of his own vocabulary. They were never even together, not really. Maybe he was drunk too, which opened a window of opportunity to act out-of-character, a window that could result in him having sex. Great. Except not great, because he wasn't keen on Jade; she was too loud and you never felt safe kidding around with her, as she was prone to twisting a joke the wrong way, taking it personally. The boy did his best to shrug her head off his shoulder but she wouldn't budge, nuzzled in deeper. Hot breath on his neck. Maybe he didn't need sex to be whole. Lots of cool people didn't have sex…

…monks. Why could he only think of monks? Surely there was ONE openly-celibate lead guitarist out there? Nope. Tank empty: monks and nobody else. Oh, and the Pope. He didn't want to be a monk or a pope though, just normal. If he remained a sexual freak, he'd never be able to have a girlfriend. Unless he somehow befriended a female sexual freak. Maybe, oh-please-god-if-you-exist, this was just a phase and he'd get over it. Yeah. Maybe he could make himself snap out of it.

He put his arm around Jade and kissed her nose. She sought out his lips. None of their friends were watching. In eighty years they'd all be dead, Facebook pages falling silent one by one. For now though, he was alive. Technically. Two slugs copulating in his mouth. Could Jade taste his fillings? If she had a nut allergy, would the Snickers bar he'd had at lunch kill her? And if this went on for much longer, would he vomit in both their mouths? He fixated his gaze beyond the field's edge, on the motorway running alongside, its steady swish of headlights. He wondered whether the people stowed inside each car were in a big hurry to get somewhere, or if it just seemed that way. A few feet off, someone tried to dance and nearly fell over; people were clapping and laughing.

The boy had never felt so alone.

# THE TASTE OF BURNT MACKEREL

*Ralph Bullivant*

Time clicks on but every so often a mote of dust will work its way against the cogs and those clicks stop for a while. These are moments that might take you for the rest of your life, fractions of time, that will colour and shade you forever.

Miriam Black-Fore would try and put those moments back together as she sat in her metal chair next to the round table on the patch of lawn that ran from the yellow door of the Cottage down to the sea. She knew where they started and how they ended but the hours in-between were no more than a wisp of spider's web. She drummed her fingers against the top of the table as if the steady sound could take back the years and those caught few hours she had lost.

One way or other Miriam owned and lived in the Cottage in West Cork for 43 years before she sold it in 1978 to Tony Moore and his wife. She was responsible for the creation of the lawn that runs down to the stone beach and the sea. Before that the Cottage stood on its scrub of rough rock raised up slightly above the pier.

A low wall was built up from the beach and rocks and stones were crushed and filled in the space behind to form a smooth surface up to the Cottage and it was then filled with good top soil brought down from the hills. They were able to pack it deep enough on the western boundary to the sea so that a few rough trees could be planted and fix down their roots. Grass was laid out over the soil and to everyone's surprise it took quickly and formed a thick green apron from the Cottage down to the sea.

When it was done and the grass had settled she bought the small round metal table and two metal chairs. These were placed on the grass outside the yellow door and she could sit there watching the water with half an eye on the iron gate to her left and the world as it passed slowly on the road.

Before the war she had friends from London. They were people she had met at university. They were artists and poets, writers and dreamers. They would come stay in the summer arriving in a smart car driven up from Cork. If they were bored they would stay for months at a time filling the Cottage with their talk and laughter. Miriam's cook and housekeeper lived in the Butter House across the road and the food would be driven in from Bantry, cooked and carried across the road to the Cottage no matter the weather.

For an evening they would sometimes walk up to Arundel's Pub where they would drink pints with the men, the farmers and fishermen, and the talk would go on deep into the night. But with the start of the war in London the visitors stopped.

It was young Donough Cronin who saw it first. It was early summer. He and the family lived in a cottage on the old road to Kilcrohane on the way to Rossekerrig. It is high there and there is a good view across the bay. He was ten at the time and was up early on some job with the hens and he looked out over the bay and there was a grey boat there low in the water stopped out beyond Owen Island. There were pictures in the papers and he recognised it as a submarine. There was a rubber boat that had been let down from the side and five men were rowing towards the pier.

Donough forgot about the hens and he shouted back in the house for his brothers and his father and then he ran down to the pier. The pier was small then, about half the length it is now and there was no slipway to pull the boats up.

By the time he got there a group of men from the village stood at the head, Tom Arundel was there and Dennis O'Mahony and a few others. Two of them had their shotguns although they kept them low down. Together they walked to the head of the pier and they watched as the rubber boat rowed up to the end.

There was no telling if the five men in the dinghy were English or German. They wore dark jackets and each of them had a thick beard. Even as they were pulling in Donough said you could see they were tired and anxious to get their feet on the ground. They tied the boat at the end of the pier and the five men climbed the metal steps to the top of the pier and the men from the village and the men from the boat faced each other.

It was Dennis O'Mahony who spoke first and he asked them

if they had been out on the water for long.

The men from the boat looked older than their years. They wore heavy wool trousers and jumpers under their black jackets. Before they started to speak they put their black hats on and the men from the village saw the German marks on them. There was a leader; he spoke in German at first and then, when he saw they didn't understand, he said in broken English, 'It is okay. We stay here a day to rest?'

Dennis O'Mahony waved a hand back over the empty bay, 'There's no permission needed here. You stay to rest if you want to.'

The men from the village walked back down the pier but they didn't go home. They hung back to see what the men from the boat would do. Donough sat down at the side of the pier and put his legs down over the edge his feet above the water.

The men from the boat talked for a while and two of them got back in their dinghy and took it back out onto the water. Their leader, he must have been the Captain, and the other two walked back down the pier and up again and their steps grew lighter as they went as if the weight of the boat was being lifted from them. As Donough was sitting there they said something to him in German and they laughed at him. Donough looked back at their dark beards and their lined faces and their clear blue eyes.

Dennis O'Mahony went to knock on the door of the Cottage and he spoke to Miriam to tell her what had gone on. She came out on the pier and the men from the boat looked surprised to see this tall woman. She walked up to them and there was more surprise when she started to speak to them in German.

She asked them questions and the Captain answered her and he seemed pleased to be able to explain where they had come from. Miriam then spoke to Dennis O'Mahony and told him they had been away at sea for three weeks and they were on their way back home. There was a problem with the boat they needed to work on and so they wanted to stop for a day in the quiet before they went back to their fighting.

'There's no bother about them,' she said.

Two more rubber dinghies came out from the boat and soon there were another twelve men on the pier. They left some back on the boat and they waved at each other. It was a still warm day and they were hot in their woollen trousers and jumpers. One of the men pulled off his heavy clothes and dived into the sea from the end of the pier. He swam out into the water gasping at how cold it was and shaking his head shouting at others to join him. Some of them did and soon most of them were in the water, enjoying the freedom of it all, their white bodies in the water.

The Captain kept away from his men. Watching them and watching the men from the village.

It was like walking into another world for the men from the boat. Locked up in their tin can for weeks at a time sinking ships and being hunted and then to be out in the sun and the light and splashing and playing games in the water. During the day some of them went back to the boat and others came back so they took it in turns. The Captain stayed by the pier and the men from the village went on their way.

The Captain went to knock on the door of the Cottage and he spoke again to Miriam and after a while they sat down on the metal chairs in her garden and they carried on talking. Miriam talked about time she had spent in Berlin before the war and the people she had known there.

After they had spoken Miriam walked up to the pub and spoke to Tom Arundel and he then came down to the pier with a tray of pints. There was no talk of how they were paid for. The pints were drunk quickly and the Captain then spoke to his men. There were more trays that came down that afternoon but the drinking of them slowed.

It was hot through the day and as the afternoon moved along some of the men from the boat slept out in the sun and their pale bodies coloured and went red. The tiredness lifted from them and the water washed away the lines in their faces.

A dinghy was taken out for fishing and they came back with two buckets of mackerel. One of the men spoke to Miriam and she spoke to Donough and asked him to fetch a pot of cream. He did that and handed the pot to the German. He was holding a thick grey root. He cut off a small nick and gave it to Donough to taste. He bit down on it and then spat it out as the heat from the horseradish caught at his nose and made his eyes water.

The German laughed and then took a sharp knife and cut at the root on a stone. Peeling it and chopping it down to a mash his eyes watering as he went. He mixed all that with the cream.

The German sailors built their fire on the raised bit of ground on the western side of the Cottage overlooking the sea. They built it with firewood gathered from the beach and the flames rose clear and high in the early evening. There was no metal grill to cook the fish on but one of the men threaded a long thin stick through the head of the mackerel so they were lined up down it and two of them held this over the embers, lifting it as the oils from the fish ran down and flared the fire.

The fish were done when they were able to gently twist away the body from the head. The cooked fish were put to one side, the heads taken off the stick and thrown to the gulls and more fresh fish were threaded on. They were able to position the fish so the stick was not exposed to the heat and that way they were able to stop it from burning. They ate them with their fingers dipping the fillets that they pulled away with their fingers in the creamy hot sauce. As the light faded from the sky the sailors' voices were quiet.

Miriam stood back and watched them from the garden. The flow of pints from the pub had stopped now but the men had been able to exchange something for two bottles of whiskey. She heard later that the pub had acquired two large glass jars of sauerkraut and a bag of smoked sausage. The sausages were eaten but the jars of sauerkraut stayed in the back of the pub for another fifteen years before they were lost.

The Captain took a plate with two mackerel and a spoon full of cream and offered it, with courtesy, to Miriam. She thanked him and took the plate. The skin of the mackerel was black and burnt. Standing there she held the plate in one hand and pulled away at the skin with her other revealing the thin white fillets. The skin had protected them from the flames and they were sweet with the sea. The sharpness of the horseradish had been dampened by the cream but it still cut through the oil in the fish. Small pieces of black skin stayed with the fillets and through it all she could taste the astringent work of the fire and its wood.

The Captain was back with his men and she stood there alone eating the two fish.

Once all the fish had been cooked the long thin stick was thrown on the fire. One of the men was down on the beach gathering dried seaweed. When this went onto the fire it flared high again and there were loud cracks as the pockets of air in the sea wrack burst. The seaweed was still damp and the men cursed as thick white smoke blew in the breeze. But the fire settled again and the shouts quietened and the men seemed embarrassed by the noise they had made in the dark.

The sun had gone down now behind the hulk of Rosskerrig and in front of them over the bay they could see the light of the moon rising up over the hills of The Mizen.

The Captain came back now to talk to Miriam. He asked her how the fish were and she told him they were good. She'd not had them with horseradish before and she didn't know the German for it. The Captain was pleased that she liked it and as the evening settled they spoke some more.

As the years went by she found it more and more difficult to piece together what they had talked about. She was never to speak German again and as the memory of the language faded away so did the memory of what they had said. She knew there had been some common ground with the places she had gone to and there was a family she had met through a student where he said there was some connection.

It maybe that the words she was trying to remember had been left unsaid.

She thought it was some time since he had really spoken to anyone. After a while they sat at the metal chairs next to the round table and they had a glass of whiskey. On the beach some of the men were singing their voices quiet now in the dark. The talk from the other men softened and they were silent listening to the half murmured songs.

She and the Captain carried on talking and she could sense the relief in him, the weight lifted, his voice in the dark.

There came a point when all was quiet from the beach and this seemed to rouse the Captain. He knew it was time to go. They sat there in silence for a while. Across the bay they could hear the sound of discordant gulls the noise rising and falling.

When he spoke again there was a change to the tone of his voice and it cut through the few moments of intimacy that had been created there in the dark. He explained that he would have to go back to the boat. He would need to be there for the night and tomorrow they would have to go back home. He thanked her for her help over the day and with a smile he thanked her for the use of the beach. He had to go back, but would she mind if some of the men were to sleep outside?

They stood up and walked down to the beach. Most of the men were awake and the Captain spoke quietly amongst them. Some of the men got up and made their way back to the pier and six of them stayed on the beach. They moved closer to the fire and put their heads back amongst the stones to watch the night sky and the stars.

The Captain looked Miriam out in the garden. He was formal now, taking his leave, shaking her hand and bowing slightly in goodbye.

He was back early next morning waking the men on the beach. They were wet with dew. The men from the village gathered again to watch them go and there was some shaking of hands. Miriam spoke in a low voice to the Captain and then they all rowed themselves back to the boat.

Donough watched as the men like small insects out there pulled at the ropes and he said you could hear the thump of its engine as it started and the boat moved out of the bay.

When the war finished Miriam asked some questions about the boat and it seemed it never got home.

Miriam had the Cottage to herself and her housekeeper across the road. Miriam would spend long days sat in her metal chair by the small round table. She wrapped herself in rugs and blankets and quietly watched the sea and the sky.

The silence was empty and then filled again, the layers of grey cloud rubbing at the landscape until all that was left was a white wall of air as if the bleached wall of some ancient church had come down and enveloped the bay. She kept herself still and the air was sepulchral around her.

# THE SHOT

*Max Dunbar*

Her husband drove her to The Didsbury in Didsbury Village, and she clockwatched the whole way; it was important to be slightly late, but then Veneesh would no doubt be late in turn. How to ensure that you did not spend a second on a table alone, checking your iPhone, avoiding the stares of predatory afternoon drinkers while you waited for the other woman?

'Yeah, UNISON gave me a grand.' Craig prated into a handsfree. 'As far as youth work goes, that's about the limit, but if you come up with a new angle they can go up to five grand.' XFM Manchester played in the background, it surprised her that he could even hear himself over that garbage. 'No, I'm on a workshop. Panatine Village Hall. Two hundred a time these guys are paying.' Indulgent, complicit laughter. 'Anyway, mate, I'll see you.' He had parked by this time and turned to his wife, and asked: 'So who's this you're meeting?'

She had the door open by now. 'Venetia Ingle, you must remember? She was in a lot of trouble.'

The name meant something to Craig, but not enough, so Vicky related the whole story: involvement in local paedo ring, underage pregnancy via a known sex offender, suicide attempt, finally a drunken stage invasion of the World Wide Message Tribe's set at Assembly that had led to her expulsion from Marple Hall. As far as Vicky knew, no one had heard from the girl for almost fifteen years, until she had resurfaced on social networking sites, and contacted Vicky through her Facebook page (on which shots of Craig and Vicky's wedding in the Tatton Marriott and honeymoon in Las Vegas were displayed, subtle yet prominent, on the photo reel).

'Yeah, I think I remember something.' Craig conceded. 'Poor kid.'

'It's the least I can do to meet her.' Her voice almost trembled with the magnanimity of it all.

'Okay, well I'll buzz back later, have a drink.' He kissed her, closed the door, and was gone in an abrasive U-turn and a blast of Mumford and Sons.

Most of Venetia's Facebook photos had been of indistinct nightclub scenes and strange foreign landscapes, so Vicky did not recognise her until the other woman waved her down. Veneesh greeted her with enthusiasm; she must have been looking forward to this for days, barely slept with the anticipation of company, probably been there for half an hour already.

The two hugged and exchanged clean, almost contactless kisses. Vicky was a little taken aback at how clean and warm Veneesh smelled. She wondered if there was a support worker, to help her wash, lend her makeup, choose her clothes. 'Hey, thanks so much for coming,' Venetia said. 'Must have freaked you out, me getting in touch out of nowhere like that!'

'Oh, Facebook is like a school reunion,' Vicky said. 'Pretty much everyone's on there. And I'm glad you got in touch.' They may have been in different leagues at Marple Hall, but Vicky didn't mind sharing an hour of her time. After all, school was a long time ago!

Her remark got them into the where-are-they-now stage. It's an iron social law that people who went to school together, no matter what their relations at the time, will bond like soul brothers when they talk as adults of their classmates' adult fortunes, and this afternoon at the Didsbury was no exception. Vicky herself kept assiduous track of the class of '98, with particular attention given to those who had got divorced, been made redundant, developed substance problems, or committed suicide. The time passed in laughter and discussion.

The pub by this time was quite crowded, but Venetia drew a waiter's attention with a speed and ease that was disconcerting. She ordered an expensive-sounding bottle of wine, and pronounced the syllables with impeccable precision, even a hint of a Mediterranean accent. Veneesh saw something in her face, and smiled. 'A little indulgence, I thought, for two ladies on a Saturday afternoon.'

'Well, why not?' Vicky felt a little flustered, which was not like her. She wondered whether to offer to pay for the wine. She wondered too long and the moment passed.

'So, how are *you*? I heard about the wedding, of course… fit Craig Mullen! I suppose that was always on the cards, since the *Grease* cast party.'

Craig had been fit, was still fit today, though Vicky did not mention or even think about the thinning, at twenty-nine, of her husband's crown, the unspecified Arts Council projects involving weekends away and last-minute overnighters, or the strange whinnying noise he made at climax, a noise that often kept her awake long after he had gone into sleep. 'Yes, we were quite the power couple, I suppose. But we both wanted to go to university, and, you know –'

Veneesh leaned in. She could smell something. Surely not perfume? The woman's eyes sparkled, and Vicky thought, she's crazy, she's only through half a glass. This is what they call a relapse. I'll have to take her to A & E. 'Sow your wild oats.'

'You could call it that!' They laughed at this, and Vicky was suddenly reminded of the other things she'd done at school, all the old magic, snogging games in the youth club or the All Saints graveyard, White Lightning or 20-20 passed from hand to hand. Where had Venetia been all those years? At home carving up her arms. Or being hand-to-handed in some Ancoats flat around men in combat gear.

'So what are you doing now? Work wise?'

'I'm a manager at Stockport Homes.'

Venetia raised an eyebrow. 'Like, council housing?'

'An ALMO.' Vicky felt a little self-conscious. Most people she socialised with knew the sector inside out. 'I allocate housing to families in need.'

Venetia leant in again, fingers propped on chin. 'So what does that involve?'

It was a source of pride to Vicky that at just twenty-eight she had worked her way up to a position where she almost never had to speak to Stockport Homes tenants, visit their overcrowded properties or even drive through the areas where the company had stock. Add that salary to Craig's youth management work and ACE income and for their age the Mullens were doing well, although perhaps not well enough for the child they were insistent on bearing.

'I mean, the Coalition's cuts don't seem to have affected us, although it's all the unions talk about,' Vicky said. 'So how about you? Do you work?'

But Venetia was lost in the menu. 'Hey, where are my manners! I must offer you lunch.'

Relief. Avoided the question. Probably on ESA for anxiety or something. Now the coalition *will* hit her hard. 'Of course, but let me pay.'

The offer was timely and clear, yet Venetia was already talking to the waiter. It was the same waiter who had brought the wine, and Vicky thought he seemed a little too attentive. Also, she had noticed men checking out their table, and she knew from a decade of street evaluations that it was not Vicky herself that they were looking at. Why? Venetia was too skinny, the hair all over the place, the skin too dark, the lips so full as to be ostentatious. Is that what men go for?

She had planned to be at the golf club by three, but here was another unexpected thing, if you please: she was enjoying Venetia's company. The woman made her laugh, and made Vicky herself feel like she was special, which is half the secret of amiability. Vicky found she didn't want to leave because she was hanging on the stories of New York and EMI deals too much to wonder how Venetia should be able to afford trips to New York or attract EMI deals. The woman had ordered steak and haloumi ('I do this at home, you must come over') a marvellous combination that should have left Vicky sluggish and listless, but somehow did not. She was thinking of university, when it had been acceptable to drink on a sunny afternoon, and laugh with your friends. The bottle ran out. Veneesh ordered another.

From her bag Venetia's mobile went off – an expensive iPhone like Vicky's own, not the pre-war Nokia that had been anticipated and hoped for. Veneesh picked it up. 'Yeah, just in the Didsbury. An old school friend, you don't know her. Come down if you like.' She clicked off. 'My partner – as you say – will be joining us. I hope you don't mind.'

The carelessness fell from her day and she knew there wasn't much time. 'I hope you don't mind me asking, Venetia, but what is it you do?'

It was the first awkward moment between them. Venetia

looked at her for a second that felt like a minute and said, 'I work at the Christie's. I'm a consultant cardiologist.'

£50,000 a year, Vicky thought. At least that. She looked at the pinstripe skirt, the cashmere that had been taken for charity-shop and clothes-collection material. 'Well, that's, that's –'

'Are you surprised, Vicky? I suppose you must be. Considering what happened. But there are resits. The Ridge did evening classes. It's possible to come back from things. Not easy, but possible.' There was a steel in her voice that hadn't been there before, not all those years as a girl, not today as a woman. 'The past is over, Vicky Beresford – or is it Vicky Mullen-Beresford now? Well, whoever you are, this is what happens next.'

A man walked into the bar, and Vicky knew even before he greeted them that this was Venetia's partner, who was not just fit like Craig but actually beautiful. Vicky had never before met a man that she could say that about.

Venetia and her man talked about public health issues and recent media cases. Vicky tried to finish her drink so that she could leave. She had almost made it when Craig appeared.

'So you must be Venetia?' A brief hug, and a handshake of congratulation and concession for the boyfriend. 'What have you guys been talking about?'

'School days.' It was the first time Vicky had spoken in half an hour.

'The best days, hey? The best days of our lives. Any more for any more?' On the heels of that Craig turned to the bar, and so missed the look of horror, of mortal fear, that came over his wife's face.

# DART TIMES

*Rory Gleeson*

'Ladies and Gentlemen, I regret to inform you that we have been delayed. Iarnród Éireann apologise for any inconvenience caused.'

The driver's voice was sharp and abrupt North Dub, though he was trying to affect the diplomatic, lilted tones of RTÉ. The train was parked up between Clontarf Road and Connolly, only four carriages at three in the afternoon. The day, grim and weepy, pattered the carriage windows with rain, new channels leaking into each other and forming rivers with each fresh drop. On the right side was the grey of Croke Park, lying in horizon at the end of the tiled plateau of terraced flats. The left faced out towards the canal.

The French couple, replete with appropriate rain gear and matching winter boots, looked about, stunned. 'What did he say?' The carriage remained silent. 'Are we stopped, how can this be, we are late already?… Excuse me, what did he say?'

Seanín, quietly poking at the goose pimples on his exposed white biceps looked up, and waited for someone else to address the question. He scanned the carriage, trying not to shiver in his t-shirt. He was freezing, but dammit he looked good. Only the tightest of t-shirts adequately cut off the blood supply around his biceps so his veins bulged and his shoulders looked like they could lift a large donkey clear of a mid-height fence. No-one else was saying anything. The young mother nearest the couple tensed on the edge of her chair, her four year old had his gaze lasering out the window, looking at a wall or a person or whatever it was four year olds looked at. To speak would be to distract him. To distract him would be to raise the devil. For the moment he just popped out every few seconds with 'Mammy, look a bike. Mammy look… A bike. Mammy, there's a cow over there. Mammy is that a river? Mammy my bum hurts. Mammy, why? Mammy my bum hurts. Mammy.' Mammy could deal with this, could convert his insistent questioning into so much static. But if he with the sore bum stopped looking out his window, got bored with the rain trickling down, the resulting rampage she could not nod away.

As the mother did not answer, Seanín leaned round the head of the chair in front to get a clear view of the attractive couple and coughed. Hmhmm. Everyone was paying attention… 'I'm sorry, sorry yeah, the driver just said we're a bit delayed, we'll be moving soon.'

'Excuse me? I did not understand you just now.' Silence raged through the carriage. He had spoken too quickly.

'Sorry, I just said that we're delayed. The train. The train driver said we're delayed, we'll be moving shortly.'

'Thank you', the two sets of magnificent white teeth shone back. The train was even quieter now, and Seanín hid quickly behind his earphones. Silence resumed, and the percussion of rain calmed down just enough for the inmates to notice they'd been relying on it.

The empty man in the hoody stood alone beside the door, his cap tilted to his eyebrows inside the hood, and his hands in his pockets, his eyes wandering in the direction of Croke Park.

He's probably looking for something to steal from those houses, came the voice of Margaret to herself. The state of the man, he hadn't met a bar of soap in days, she reckoned. Look at him there, she bet he did drugs as well. Men over the age of thirty had no call to be wearing tracksuits. Well if he tried to take her bag he'd have another thing coming. By God, he'd not dealt with the likes of Margaret Daly before. She had heard the best way to deter muggers at her age was to make an advance on them before they could start their nonsense. Embarrass them out of the idea of robbing you. If it came down to it, Margaret would have no problem using this method. She glared at the man, and started clawing through her handbag for the bright red lipstick she had for social gatherings and emergencies.

Eoin moved his head beneath the blue hood so that his perspective of a single rain drop on the window changed. It appeared as if either the drop was moving or the houses behind were moving, so he busied himself by walking the raindrop up and down the streets outside, sometimes making it call into houses or start breakdancing in the street. After a few moments he realised his head was vibrating as he made the drop twirl faster and faster and he stopped. That must have looked weird. He looked about the carriage, some foreigners, lady with a baby, young lad looking at his muscles, decent looking bird in the corner, hmm, old lady watching him. The lady was pouting her lips at him and thrusting her bosom in his direction. He cautiously turned away. What the hell was wrong with her? Dirty auld one. He needed to get off the train. Quick. He looked about again, and spotted the legs of the girl propped up against the back of an empty chair. Pity with all the tights being worn these days. The leaders of the fashion world had decided that Eoin would have to work a bit harder to see skin on display, and he found this, frankly, unfair.

Emily nipped at the ladder in her tights. She was using the window to see beyond the head of a chair at the far end of the carriage. It allowed her to see around to the face of the young man with the ear phones. God he was gorgeous. She bet he'd take care of you. He'd take you places, not just like to his house for a bit of TV. He'd probably bring you to the theatre. He'd look brilliant in a suit as well. Pure class, like. And look at those muscles on him. Jesus, she'd say he could lift you up in the air like Patrick Swayze. And he was good to those people when they asked a question. Oh, she'd be on him in a second if she met him in a club. She wondered if he noticed her, he was always looking down at himself, probably because he was such a deep thinker. She'd been on the same train with him a few times, and had been looking better every morning since the second time she saw him. Perfume was no longer reserved for nights out. Nothing wrong with some Chanel in the morning, she'd told Daddy. Oh wouldn't it be brilliant if he came over to talk to her, asked her out. Why did she have to wait for him though? She'd looked at him plenty, when their eyes caught she'd throw them away really quickly, and then look back slyly a few seconds later, but he'd be back looking down at himself. Why couldn't she ask him out? Ask him his name? But oh, what if he was really boring, or a weirdo or something. What if he threw the lips on her straight away, would she let him or tell him to wait a bit? What if she did let him, then he turned out to be a serial cheater or something? What if he had a girlfriend actually, she had never thought of that. Or what if he was just not interested and asked her to go away? Too much, too much. Right, that's grand, leave him where he was, and maybe just sit closer to him the next time, put on a bit more perfume, he'd be round eventually. It was cold, thank god she was wearing tights.

Margaret gazed at Emily's long legs. God she'd love to have legs like hers again. Emily pouted at Seanín, oh wasn't he beautiful. Seanín looked at himself, his arms looked good. The mother peered away from little Jimmy, oh please would he shut up. Eoin glinted at Emily, she'd a nice face. Emily lowered her eyes, was he on drugs? Little Jimmy stared at Margaret, you're old, look mammy she's old. Mammy smiled at the French couple, never have children. French people cuddled each other, je t'aime, et tu, je t'aime aussi. The thoughts of the carriage swirled up and down the aisles in a maelstrom of captured madness. Everyone pretending to be normal, or busy, but no one being either. They were all stuck together, they had been since Margaret got on at Raheny, but no one had noticed. Stuck, together. Nothing new but the change in rain and which foot Eoin placed his weight on. Left right left. He hopped from one to the other, and nothing new there in itself. How would they get out, surely the train could feel what was going on in its body and stop this, stop the rain, stop the view, stop the sky from getting darker and the lips of Margaret getting redder. Something must end soon, this could not continue, and as the heat drained from the train and rose through Mammy's face, she parried Jimmy's clawing hands, the shiver in Emily's legs growing thicker and Seanín's arms getting colder, could it not stop, why weren't they moving, why weren't they moving?

'Ladies and Gentlemen I'd like to apologise once more for this delay. Iarnród Éireann apologise for any inconvenience caused.'

The mic crackled and scuffled as it was replaced. They looked at each other again, the tension beginning to mount once more, each thinking in their own way how they were different, why they weren't normal. Then, without warning, came the sound of a four year old in dungarees reaching critical mass.

'Aaaaaaaaaaaaaaahhhhhhhh,' Jimmy sprang from the edge of his seat, no longer happy with the window. He evaded mammy's grabbing hands and charged down the middle of the train, his arms straight out on either side of his shoulders. 'Nnneeeeeeeeeeeeeer, I'm a plane I'm a plane.' Mammy rolled from her chair after him in pursuit, a controlled rage in a sharp step, knowing he was running out of space. Jimmy reached the end of the carriage, and looked up at Emily, who smiled awkwardly at him. 'Look, go to your mammy, your mammy's after you, go to her there.' 'You're weird.' He scrambled under mammy's legs and threw himself back down to the other end of the carriage. He ran by Margaret, who gave a little 'oh'. 'Neeeeeeeer,' he passed by Eoin who was pretending not to notice, then by his own table in the middle of the carriage, by the French couple, who muttered something about child rearing practices, and down the other end where Seanin sat. 'Neeeeeeeeerrr.' Seanin looked powerless to help, nothing his big muscles could do. 'Mammy I'm bored, and now I'm an airplane. Neeeeeeer.' Mammy was still down the other end of the carriage holding her head in her hands, the frustration boiling through her body towards her face, destined to make tears if much more continued. Lack of sleep had stopped her muscles from being able to grab four year olds the way they should, and skipping breakfast had scuttled her mental strength. She was on the edge, one more unscheduled flight would do it. Tears would come, and may not be stopped, and Jimmy would then forever know that he could win. At four years of age, he'd be alpha, and then he'd probably end up a drug dealer or something. Jimmy was revving up his engines, somewhere between a rocket ship and a formula one car and was beginning to take off. 'Nnnnnnnnnnnnneeeeeeee.' Seanín wished so much his earphones were attached to something, Eoin was ready to smash his way off the train. Jimmy's baby steps began, he was gathering speed and decibels and was planning an assault right at the shins of mammy, who would have been defenceless by the time he reached top speed. Neeeeeeer-

Stop. A hand and arm came out from behind a chair into the middle of the aisle. Jimmy hadn't been expecting it, and his noise dropped off as he skidded a bit to avoid the odd coloured hand blocking his way. He followed the manicured nails left to the long thin fingers leading to a tweed jacket, and traced the green brown lines back to the body and face of an old man. His dark eyes measured Jimmy up and down, who understood he was involved in something. Four year olds can smell social conflict, and know how to behave in a battle for hierarchy. He demanded explanation for his cancelled flight. 'I'm an airplane.'

'I know you are.' The carriage jolted. A hissing as people began shifting in seats to get a better look, jerking and creaking as they tried to see around headrests, handle bars and pram handles. He pressed his advantage, 'It's just that you can't take off in here because there's a roof. You'd crash into it. We'd have to take you to the hospital.' Jimmy wouldn't give up that easy, though something in the man's layered, grooved face suggested he knew what he was talking about. Mammy was treading slowly back to Jimmy, closing in, stalking him down before he could move again. The man held Jimmy's attention who didn't notice mammy creeping up on him.

'I don't care about the hospital.'

'Oh I know you don't, you're a brave boy, you're a pilot.'

'I'm an airplane.'

'Oh yes, you're an airplane, but even airplanes don't want to go to hospital. In hospital they make you stay in bed all day, and you can't go outside and run around.'

'I don't care about that.' Jimmy was defiant, but slowly in his mind, he reminded himself, he loved to be outside. Outside had leaves and everything.

'You don't? Oh but who doesn't like to be outside. In hospital they don't let you outside, and they make you eat vegetables.'

'Euch.'

'Euch is right. Yes I know, vegetables, green ones, yucky ones. And they don't let you play guns, and you can't watch cartoons.'

'No cartoons?' Jimmy was losing, what kind of place would ban cartoons? Mammy was gaining ground, she was almost there.

'Well they have cartoons, but you only have one television, so you have to watch something everyone wants to watch.'

'What do you watch then?'

'Oh, something like the news.'

'EEEEW.' The news was rotten, the news was boring, Mammy watched it all the time and she made him be quiet for it, and if he wasn't quiet he had to go to his room and be quiet, or worse, play with his sister. This man had it right, who wanted to watch the news?

'Ew, I know, it's awful. So you don't want to be a plane on a train, in case you end up in hospital and have to watch the news every day.'

'No.' Jimmy gazed right up at the man again, who looked back. Black eyes he had, surrounded by weird-looking skin, but he couldn't look away. He calmed him down, made him peaceful. Perhaps he could be Jimmy's new pet, his best friend. But now he was looking to the side of Jimmy's head, looking at something behind him. The old man grinned, a toothy smile. Something was wrong.

'Oh look, it's your mammy.'

Before he could react Jimmy was grabbed up by the scruff of his shirt. 'Got ya! Never. Do that again.'

As he was hoisted back to his seat. Jimmy howled, betrayed, ensnared. 'No! Aaaaah no!' His brief moment of freedom had been caught up by the old man in that seat, he'd been led astray, his path diverted by subterfuge and trickery. Deceit! Lies! The old man smiled at Jimmy being taken away.

'Thanks a million,' Mammy stressed, as she hoofed the wriggling prisoner under her arm. He smiled again,

'No problem, love. I've learned a trick or two in my time.'

'C'mon Jimmy now.' Jimmy kicked half-heartedly all the way back, the disobedient cub in the jaws of the mother lion. He stared at the man from under mammy's arms. The old man waved at him, 'Bye Jimmy.' Led back to a window seat, and trapped by his mother's body. He sulked, and replayed how he had been lied to and his freedom taken from him. Bet they don't even make you watch the news in hospital. Mammy was grateful, and now had the justification to tell him to be quiet. He had been bold, so he had relinquished talking privileges.

The French couple smirked at the child, and everyone went back to what they were doing, pretending they had never stopped doing it in the first place. Emily began to search again for Seanín in the window, but the train rumbled and shook and started to move slowly along the tracks. The view changed and shifted, Croke Park ducked out of sight behind some closer houses, and Connolly platform approached as crackling came over the intercom.

'Ladies and Gentlemen we're getting moving now. We should be arriving in Connolly station shortly. Iarnród Éireann would like to apologise for any inconvenience this slight delay has caused. Thank you and safe journey.'

Emily took her legs down, and gave herself a quick spray of Chanel. He'd have no chance after this.

# KILLER

*Anthony Howcroft*

In ten minutes I'll be dead. Nobody will notice.

'They've found Veronica Martin's body,' Steve growls.

The name is familiar but I can't place it. I'm getting paranoid about my memory as I get older. I stare at Steve's square face, wondering if I might gather a clue about Veronica's identity. Steve looks the same as when we were at school. I don't. I'm losing hair and gaining weight in some kind of inverse proportional relationship.

'She was stuffed into a plastic box,' Steve says. 'They found it at the bottom of a cesspit by Nether Thorpe.'

'Steve.' Amy gives him a look. 'We're eating.'

He shrugs and forks a scallop into his mouth.

We don't see Steve and Amy very frequently. Our friendship is a little rusty, but worth lubricating with wine and good food every so often. I have eight minutes of life remaining.

'I can't believe you missed it,' Amy says.

'I never bother with the news.' I reply.

My wife shudders. 'The news is so depressing. They only cover the recession, middle east wars, murder and abducted children, and themselves.' she collects the plates. Then I remember Veronica. Relief is my primary response.

It means I haven't succumbed to Alzheimer's yet, like my mother.

Veronica Martin was at our school. She had a boyish face with a warm smile that was quirky, off-centre but full of laughter. Her hair was short, dark brown with a kiss-curl that fell over her forehead. Physically she was small and curvy, yet still athletic and loose-limbed in her own way. I liked her. She wasn't a fashionable person to be attracted to but she had a unique quality. Veronica disappeared when we were sixteen. The story was all over the national papers. Her parents gave the press one of those school photos that looked nothing like the girl we knew. It was splattered everywhere for weeks.

I open another bottle of wine and refill the decanter. We don't use it normally and it makes me feel like a stranger in my own home.

Veronica would be an adult now. I remember the joke.

*What's the difference between Elvis and Veronica?*

*Most people think Elvis is still alive.*

'Veronica Martin,' I say. The words feel strange. 'It's frightening how quickly we forget. Life steamrollers forward.'

'What else can you do?' Steve replies.

I go upstairs to check on my daughter. I leave Amy and Steve debating the etiquette of raising gruesome topics during dinner. I try the stiff door into my daughter's room. The handle sticks really badly and you have to apply a lot of force. If I weren't so useless at DIY I'd have made an attempt to fix it.

She's fast asleep with her bear cuddled tightly under one arm. She looks like an angel. My wife hates it when I say that. She doesn't like the association, angel equals dead in her way of thinking. I close the door and return downstairs. Only a minute left before I die.

'More wine?' I say.

'Go on then.' Steve holds out his glass.

'I thought you were driving?' Amy asks.

'Not now.' Steve laughs.

I can see the plastic box. I can feel it, the weight and texture, the sticky sides. The plastic box in my hands, packed with colourful bits squeezing against the sides like a Chinese takeaway. I'm placing it at the bottom of the cesspit. I am the murderer. The memory is vivid and absolutely real. I can feel the damp morning air, smell the reek of the pit.

The person I was is dead. I'm not sure who I am.

Wait, this is impossible. I couldn't commit such an atrocious act and only realise it now. The human mind is powerful but this can't be true. Logically, this must be a hallucination – or a powerful empathetic response because I'm a father. There's no way a brain could eradicate a memory so completely from the conscious mind. It's been more than twenty years since she died. There would have been after effects, some leakage. I've never had any dreams about Veronica. No recognition from reports about similar crimes. No flashbacks until now. Tell me you don't believe this could happen. Tell me.

'Hello?' Amy says. 'Are you OK?'

'Sorry, miles away.' I say.

'Can I get a glass of water?' she asks.

'Of course,' I reply.

The water's in the utility room. I lean on the freezer and try to talk myself back into sanity. I can't have murdered someone. I would know. Anyone would.

We're not robots from a sci-fi film with reprogrammable memories. Or that guy who has to write himself notes so he knows who he is when he wakes up.

What the hell was that film called?

All the time the plastic box flashes in my head like a movie scene. Each frame clicks forward in slow motion as I bend to place the box in the sewage, keeping it horizontal so nothing spills. I don't remember killing Veronica.

Somebody must have cut her into pieces and crushed the dismembered parts into a see-through container. If I can't remember that, perhaps it wasn't me?

I clutch at this as evidence of my innocence. Yet the plastic box is compelling. I have to consider there may be other memories buried so deeply I can't recall them. I fear they'll surface soon, like Veronica.

I make a detour to my office and fire up my computer. I Google memory-loss. An Amazon book is listed, *Offenders' memories of violent crimes*. Amazon's 'Search Inside' feature lets me peer within the body of text. Jargon assaults me: post traumatic stress disorder, dissociative amnesia. I read, *there are a variety of predisposing, precipitating and perpetuating biopsychosocial factors that interact to guide an offenders' memory.*

Here's my straw. I read the sentence again. It says that memory is not fixed. So it's possible my memory is false. Something I never actually did rather than an event I've forgotten. I read on and the picture turns darker. Most violent criminals fake PTSD, amnesia or both. The book lists techniques to interrogate criminals, to catch them out and prove their guilt. The introduction finishes. Amy is waiting for her drink. My wife needs help in the kitchen. The book is out of stock with a twelve-day order period. I turn to Wikipedia and search on amnesia and violent crime. All I keep hitting are references to films.

I want a simple answer. Am I a murderer?

There's a second question: can a person be held responsible for a crime they didn't know they committed? I'm pretty sure I can guess the answer.

Diminished responsibility is a phrase you hear on the radio when lawyers contrive to get lighter sentences for their psychopathic clients. That isn't me.

I'm one of the good guys and my memory isn't diminished. It was completely missing until tonight.

My wife calls. I clear the screen and delete the history. Then I remember that Google keep the results of every search linked to IP addresses. The police probably trawl through them. I swear at my own stupidity. I need to come back later and do more searches, for their benefit and mine. Walking down the stairs I fashion other phrases I could use to show me as the victim; innocent murder, fabricated memories, paranoia, empathetic crime syndrome.

'Where have you been?' My wife whispers angrily.

'I had to check my email.'

'Now?' she looks ready to kill.

I mumble a reply and wipe my face with a tea towel. I take Amy her water with a few cubes of ice. They rattle like bones as I cross the room. I ask Steve about work and try to nod and grunt in the right places to keep him talking.

Chaos whirls through my head on a wild spree, pulling open neatly filed memories, trampling and stamping them into the floor. I'll lose everything.

Perhaps my parents can forgive me but the effort will destroy them. Friends will abandon our family in droves. Emma will be bullied at school. I'll be an outcast. A target for every violent thug wanting to thrash out his anger on someone lower in the prison hierarchy. My future is a checklist of disintegration. Then again, at least I'm not a paedophile. I mean she was only a kid but so was I. You have to be older to be a paedophile don't you?

'How's your job going?' Amy asks, when I've left too long a gap without prompting Steve.

'Good,' I say. Years of late nights hauling myself up the corporate ladder, all wasted. I imagine our beautiful home covered in graffiti and sold for peanuts to someone who doesn't care about its history as the residence of a killer. That's if they don't destroy it. I've heard the police sometimes demolish murderer's houses so nobody profits from crime. I wonder if my wife would still get an insurance pay-out. There's probably some weasel-clause that means she'll lose out.

Everything seems transparent, ghostly, although it's actually me that's fading. I can see and touch them today but they'll be taken away. This must be a mistake. I can mentally construct a way out. Think out of the box.

I know you decided very quickly that I did it, and you're repulsed. You tell yourself this can only happen in a story and it could never happen to you. I should send you that Amazon book. I know you won't order it for yourself. What if it says I'm right? That memory can be completely suppressed or created by circumstance and proven to be absolutely false. That would mean you too could be a murderer. You're in denial. You'll find a way to rationalize not purchasing the book; too expensive, not your sort of thing, too academic. I bet you don't even believe it exists. I dare you to check Amazon now. I can tell you feel entirely justified in not bothering. Your defence is a one hundred percent certainty in your identity. There are no black holes in your memories, no gaps. Which is how I felt, a few minutes ago.

My wife pops her head around the door.

'Can I borrow you?' she says. 'I need you to do some chopping.'

My wife is so busy directing the kitchen tasks she doesn't notice anything is wrong. I feel clumsy. The knife is heavy and each slice of carrot feels like a crime as it crunches and topples on the wooden board. I catch my finger.

'It's just a nick. Better run it under the tap.' She deposits a packet of Hannah Montana plasters by the sink. I hold my finger in the running water for a long time, turning it from side to side.

I'm stupid. Let's assume, hypothetically, that I'm guilty. Why would I commit such a terrible crime so badly? Why did I use a cesspit? They always get emptied. The remains were destined to surface. I left a time-bomb. Then I think of my choice of box, a see-through plastic container. How unbelievably foolish. At the very least I should have used something opaque. Even better, if I'd emptied the remains into the pit they would have decomposed. There would be nothing left after all this time. Instead, I used an airproof and watertight box that preserved everything. Each cut available for forensic analysis. Veronica's white teeth ready to check against dental records. Her DNA and mine mixed together. I might as well have left a business card. What the hell was I thinking? I was a smart kid. Yet this was amateur, like it wasn't me at all.

I manage to hold myself vaguely together during the main course, which is a herb-crusted tenderloin. Luckily my wife likes it well done, so I don't have to see any blood swilling around on my plate. Whenever the conversation heads in the wrong direction I nudge it with a question, steering the talk towards schools, nannies and that perennial favourite, which celebrities our partners would grant us a one-night pass.

An hour ago I considered myself a responsible parent. Now I'm manipulating conversations to cover up a murder. I wish everyone would leave me alone. I want to curl up in a corner.

'What do you think about Sophie?' Steve asks out of the blue. I begin to sweat. That case never seems to be out of the press, even after all this time.

Murder sweeps back as our topic, hovering above me with pointing fingers.

'I can't tell the facts from the speculation anymore. What do you think?' My wife says.

'Well,' Steve looks to Amy for approval. 'We still think they did it.'

'I hope so.' I say too enthusiastically.

Everyone looks at me.

'If they didn't we have to assume there are monsters waiting to kidnap our children when our backs are turned.'

'That's the real world.' Amy says.

'I don't believe they could hide something like that,' Susan says.

'I heard they sell ten thousand more copies with her picture on the cover,' Steve adds.

I shake my head, but secretly know I'm the first to stop and read the headline if I see her picture. I'm suddenly unsure if everyone does that.

'Rubber-neckers.' I say. 'They'd sit around the guillotine if they could.'

It's all I can do to appear normal. Maintaining a conversation is an effort that nearly makes me explode. If the police come I'm lost. I remember being interviewed last time – everyone in my class had to give a statement. That was different though as I believed I was innocent. Questioned again I'll fold. I can't lie convincingly. Not that it will matter if I'm a Machiavellian liar. The DNA evidence will be compelling. I try to remember what percentage of the population is covered on the police genetic database. I don't know if I'm on it or not. My support for civil liberties groups has never been higher.

'Excuse me for a moment,' I say.

My wife looks a little surprised as I get up part way through the course. I try to give her a reassuring gesture, rubbing her shoulder. I wander through the house and hope the police never put the pieces together. That's a bad phrase.

The garage is cooler and I get in the car and let the door hang open for a while. The smell of leather is reassuring. I could disappear. The car whispers seductively, *we could head for the coast, leave everything behind. No worries but the price of oil.* The car doesn't actually speak to me. I don't hear voices, you understand, I'm just talking metaphorically. Trouble is I have no idea how to get another passport. I would be CCTV tracked wherever I went. Would I rather my daughter never knew her father or thought of me as a monster? That's the key question. If I disappear people will want to know why. Two and two are easy numbers to put together.

Suicide is an honourable way out, if I can make it look like an accident. It would leave my family in the clear, financially secure, and they might recall me as I am now. Although, given that my daughter is not yet four will she even remember me in a few years time? My earliest memories are from six years old, I think.

My wife finds me.

'Looking for my glasses. Contact lenses have dried up,' I say.

'They're upstairs,' she answers.

When I rejoin everyone, the conversation is stuck where I left it.

'Isn't that what they say?' Steve asks. 'We're all beasts beneath a thin veneer of civilization?'

'That's what they say about men.' Amy says.

My wife remarks, 'They always get them in the end.'

Steve agrees. 'They've solved four or five cases in the last couple of months. They can grow DNA in the lab from a sample so small you can't see it. Who knows what they might do in a few years?'

'Read minds?' Amy says.

'Or predict who might commit a crime?' my wife adds.

'Like that film with Tom Cruise.' Steve grins.

'He's on my list.' Amy smiles back at Steve.

'I thought we'd banned scientologists?' He says.

After they go I help tidy up and then I check on my daughter again. You may think I'm crazy, schizophrenic, bipolar, whatever the current politically correct term is. You know I wouldn't dream of harming her. I can hear your arguments, the logic that says I'm not in control of myself. That's imperfect thinking. I'm literally a different person to twenty years ago – doesn't every part of your body rebuild each couple of years?

As we slump into bed my wife wants to know if I think it has gone well. My lacklustre response worries her.

'How well did you know Veronica?' she asks.

I mumble a reply, kiss her and rollover to sleep.

I half expect the darkness to hold nightmares, the murder replayed in full graphic detail. Blood, squelching boots, screams, hacksaws, the cesspit. Every sensation waits to pounce on me. Instead, I sleep soundly.

I awake refreshed. The sunlight filters through a crack in the curtains, producing a crystal-like prismatic display across the ceiling, until memory returns like a sledgehammer, and all I can see is red.

I think my only talent is deceit and I'm the primary victim. In the days after the party I become accustomed to my new memory. None of the other details return. I reason that I must have killed her accidentally and covered it up, a panicked teenager. It may not leave me blameless, but at least human. We're all surely allowed one mistake in our youth, however terrible.

Four days later I remember Angela Snell. I used a fire to dispose of her. The next day, well, I daren't tell you what happened to Jane Drew. You wouldn't understand.

# RELIC

## *David Martin*

No-one saw him fall from the sky the night of the strange lights. The lights themselves were only seen by the sleepless, the drunk, the late shift workers raising gritty eyes from their screens for a moment's break. And they caused only a flurry of filler in the local news, and a brief effusion of conspiracy theories gibbering to themselves in the digital dark. But he lay undiscovered for days, weeks, embedded in the soft ground by the shattering impact of his fall, in the heart of the wood in a bare and clodded field on the edge of town.

No-one was watching at the frozen hour when the lights streaked low overhead, or in their wake heard the crashing of branches and the outraged eruption of birds.

Close up you could see the marks of his descent through the canopy of trees, their broken limbs charting his passage, letting new shafts of light fall into the shadowed space where he lay, close by a silent pond. From outside the wood was undisturbed, keeping its secret. But secrets find their way out, too good to keep, but good enough to keep close.

We never saw what was inside the suit, it was still intact, but burned and battered, its identifying markings lost, the visor black and impenetrable. We liked to scare ourselves daft by imagining the broken and rotting form within. Because it was definitely occupied. You could tell by the heft and shape of it, even before one of us dared to poke it with a stick and then ran like hell after feeling something's inert bulk shift within, a sound and movement we never forgot.

Someone said he'd probably been dead for decades, a remnant from the black and white days of moonwalks and spacewalks and Sputniks, some failed long-denied Cold War mission. Maybe there was only ever a dried-out skeleton inside, empty eye sockets still haunted by the years of staring into a greater void, while the Earth in all its blue-white beauty revolved forever out of reach.

No-one was quite sure who found it first, and it was a story that seemed to choose its own initiates. Somehow each of us knew the kind of person we should confide in. We weren't all friends, came from all over town, had little else in common, yet somehow we knew to keep it secret from everyone else, even siblings, even our obvious best friends. Looking back, it was as though it could see something in each of us that we couldn't. But soon a few of us were coming down regularly, clandestinely but never alone, always with increasingly elaborate cover stories. We would cling to the grassy path at the margin of the field, scouring the horizons for any sign of the farmer, or any bigger, older, harder kids, before half-running, half-hobbling across the cold, sucking, trainer-ruining clods to the wood, to the gap in the barbed wire fencing and the path to the stagnant central pond.

Kids before us had been coming here for generations to smoke, drink, snog, screw and scare the shit out of each other with tales of the ghosts and serial killers who had of course haunted this place. They'd recorded their visits for posterity with carved and penned initials on tree trunks and fenceposts, some already fading with age. But it looked as though this spot had fallen out of favour for a good few years, ever since the new barbed wire fence went up, the gaping hole in it had been made fairly recently.

I can't remember what we did or talked about for the most part. All I can really recall is the quiet of that hidden space, the giant helmeted and booted figure prostrate in the gloom, holding all the gazes of all those people whose faces I've long forgotten. There was talk of telling, of fame and rewards, but the longer we delayed, the less convincing it became that we ever would. Soon we were talking instead about ways of keeping the secret, whether anyone suspected, and what we'd do to anyone who told. Soon it became clear that we were missing the point anyway. However secret the dead presence at the heart of the wood was, it was quietly changing us, and the world around us.

Gradually moss began to grow in the joints of the suit and cover the visor, the Earth beginning to reclaim the astronaut. And at night our dreams became filled first with the image of that inscrutable faceplate, but then the blackness behind it drew us in, opening out on to great abysses of stars. Utter silences, which once you learned to listen to them filled with the hissing of radiation from impossibly distant suns, the shiver of strange particles, the loneliness of the void.

It soon began to spill into the waking hours. Sometimes an ordinary street would seem transfigured, warped by a glimpse of some other geometry that lay beyond it, planes and spaces that defied human description. The sunlight that fell on it revealed to us its own origins in prominences like a billion nuclear wars finally unleashed, and at the same time how on this monstrous scale it was nothing, a few flecks of frozen light. A single moment of time would open up into an infinite present, becoming a pool you could plunge into and be lost, sinking through the fine grain of the universe itself towards whatever final truth might lie at the heart of things.

While space and time opened up for us, the ground accelerated its attempts to devour the astronaut. Grasses grew up around his edges. Seeds propagated in the folds of his suit, tendrils found their way into the mysterious holes for the missing hoses that once kept him alive. More than once we saw a worm emerge from a boot or gauntlet. The ditches and streams that radiated out from the wood became his nervous system, spreading whatever he'd brought back from the cosmos into the ground, the water, the air. And at the same time feeding something back to him.

It wasn't just us. We started noticing people lost in reverie, and houses with open doors, drawn curtains and abandoned cars, where the everyday routine of work and family had been replaced by far deeper, stranger rhythms. Some people never came home. We heard a rumour the minister at the Congregationalist church had started speaking in hexadecimal numbers in the middle of his lesson.

Our classes began dwindling but none of the teachers seemed that concerned, their own ranks were becoming increasingly chaotic. I don't know now if I witnessed it myself or if it was just another story, but one became stuck in a loop, intoning a stream of seeming nonsense before heading for the doorway, only to flicker instantly back to the spot she'd started from, to repeat it all over and over.

We noticed the planes gradually stopped their regular groaning overhead, diverting their flightpaths away almost unconsciously from the airspace above our town. TVs began interjecting bursts of white noise and shifting fractal patterns in between the gameshows and weather bulletins, and nobody really commented on it.

Our dreams became darker, our visits to the wood uneasier.

We began to share a dream where we saw the astronaut not lying prostrate and dead but standing upright and waiting for us with silent command. We only saw him in silhouette, a figure cut from utter blackness. In these new dreams there was something profoundly wrong about that shape, that form, it seemed an absence, not a presence, a hole punched through reality.

Every time we visited the wood now, we knew that one day we would find him standing there for real, ready to issue some unimaginable instruction.

But as we headed to the field one morning we knew it was over. Something had changed. A passenger jet droned overhead.

As we crossed the clods we saw figures moving between the trees; bigger, older, harder kids. We heard a motorbike engine and a burst of laughter as we skulked on the periphery of bushes and barbed wire, shut out from our no longer secret kingdom. Moving like shadows, worming through the trees towards the centre, we got a glimpse of someone's much-feared older brother bent over the suit, levering the faceplate off with a stick. A girl was calling out to him, half egging him on, half horrified. A twig broke. We scattered in all directions before anyone saw us, working our way back to our separate homes by our separate routes, dodging any imaginable pursuit through the town's hidden arteries of tracks and alleys.

It was hushed up what was actually found in the wood, the papers said it was a fragment of a decommissioned satellite, there were hints about classified military hardware, and that was it. Who the astronaut was and what became of him I still don't know. Decades on I couldn't tell you what became of everyone else. Like I said, we didn't have a lot else in common. And I struggle to remember anything of those glimpses into the unimaginable that the astronaut brought back.

Sometimes on a clear, quiet night, I still watch the stars. But all that's up there is a belt of dead junk, babbling satellites dumbly bouncing our own distorted reflections back at us, with entropy gnawing at every image.

It's past midnight and everyone is sleeping. A meteor slides down through Orion. Something snuffles in the field hidden behind hedges, but otherwise the night is still. I think about the darkness lying heavy across half the world, pressed up against the flimsy slats of my back fence, seeping through its gaps and cracks.

# STILLNESS

*Duncan Ross*

Ma right foot itches somewhere between the arch and the heel. If somebody were to come across it on the battlefield and scratch it, ah wonder if the feeling would go away. The phantom sensation, caused by what the physicians call 'catastrophic nerve trauma', is a permanent reminder of the choices ah made. The feeling that ma missing hand is constantly being crushed is yet one more.

Boom, bang, and that was that; or so ah thought. A third shell landed besides me, and that really was *that*. Legs, arm, joy and future were all obliterated in a flash. Ah remember trying to pick up bits o' ma self with ma remaining hand. Need that, ah thought; need that, too.

Ah lay there in the filth for what seemed like a lifetime until a fatherly voice said.

'Come on son, let's get ye out o' here.'

'Am ah no dead?' ah gurgled.

'No son. You're alive.'

What was our objective that day? to take a ridge? take a trench? Shoehorn some poor guy like maself out o' his hidey hole? The fuck do ah know about that kind ah thing? It's got nothing to do with me. Ah was there for the party. Well ah got ma party.

The last stroll ah took with ma legs, ma football legs, was across a grey brown landscape o' stinking mud and corruption; treading and stumbling over my friends' backs, faces and hands. Human bodies make for lousy paving, ah tell ye. My transport now consists o' canvas stretchers and rickety old wheeled beds and chairs. Aye, no more sprints for goal, no more tackles and no more dribbling; aside from that out o' my stupid mouth occasionally.

From the lasses ah get just as many looks as ah used tae. But where a glance would once turn into a smile and a blush, it now morphs into a mask o' pity and horror. I'm peered at like ah'm some kind o' sideshow curiosity. Take a look, girls. Aye, this is me; Campbell. Now half a man, maybe three quarters if ah'm lucky.

Meg is coming to see me later. Lewis brings her. Ma old friend Lewis who stayed behind when ah signed up.

'Ah just don't fancy it, Campbell,' he said, finishing his pint. 'Never liked the sound o' France.'

'Aye. Ye never like the sound o' nothing,' ah says to him. 'Stuck in ye ways is what ye are. Birds ah gonna love me in ma kilt. Do you no want a part o' that?'

'Ah like the highlands, Campbell; the glens; thassall.'

He's the smart one, I see now. No lured by the flash and dazzle they put before us all. No like me and the others, who swallowed the whole sham like a peg o' ale. Most of the old boys lay draped over a field in Flanders like some grotesque rotting blanket. A couple made it back. Ah see Clarke from time to time but he cannae talk no more. He's one of the so called 'broken faces'. Silence is his legacy, as stillness is mine.

Ah see the way Meg looks at Lewis and the way she looks at me. Love and pity, pity and love. Ah know full well which one is for me. Ah cannae blame her, after all, what am ah nowadays? A shadow, a memory; a whisper of what was.

Ah catch sight o' ma half arm and ma half legs. The fabric o' ma clothes is neatly folded and pinned back in a vain attempt to add some ordinariness to the spectacle. How can a person simply lose bits of oneself? ah think. It's horrifying, and they're just the wounds ye can see. I cannae explain the shattered feeling inside; and just as well because chaps don't talk about such things, or so ma dad says. Ah told the chaplain ah was fine. *Just fine.*

Ma mother came to visit me.

'Can ah have ma chance again maam? my life back?' ah plead to her.

She doesnae answer, just cries. Aw she does is cry.

It's a stupid question anyhow. 'Course ah cannae have them back. They were blown to smithereens. Both chance and life lie broken and wrecked in a foreign field.

Why didn'ae the explosion just take ma life? ah wonder. It took everything else. What's down for me now? Fuck aw, that's what. Ah just sit and stare like some perpetually stunned animal. Ah want to end it aw, but, aside from it being an unchristian act, ah'm too scared to do it. What if ah'm like this on the other side? Who'll help me?

It's pure self pity ah feel. Ah'll no hide the fact. Ah cannae help it. Ah don't want to be like this. Ah'm just a boy for Christ's sake. No a man as ah thought ah was. Just a stupid boy.

Ah watch the Hawthorns play in the park as ah once did. Ah get wheeled down there from time to time. Not too close o' course. The nurses don't like to cause a stir.

'Don't go Campbell, don't go,' ah scream inside, as ah see ma self striking the ball into the top corner o' the net. 'Think,' ah shout. But he won't think, the laughing fool; because ye don't think, Campbell. Ye never bloody think; you just *do*.

Jesus, ma foot itches so bad.

A hand gently squeezes ma shoulder.

'What ye doing there Campbell,' her soft voice says.

'Just looking back, pet.' I close ma diary.

'Don't look back too much, love. It's not always a good thing.'

She's right, o' course, but it's good to see how far ah've come sometimes.

Elizabeth folds a blanket and places on the end o' ma bed. Mesmerised, I watch her. Her hair has this beautiful little habit of not behaving and falling oot o' any style she attempts to put it into. Quietly singing, she gathers it up at the sides and clips it back into place. She puts her hands on her hips and then looks at me slightly oot o' breath.

It's curious thinking back to that first year. Those were dark days when I couldn'ae imagine a future and couldn'ae see things ever gettin' better. Elizabeth was there by ma side in ma darkest hour like ah guardian angel. Ah'd awake in the night screaming and drenched with sweat and she'd be right there holdin' ma hand in hers. Some nights ah'd be so scared ah could barely breathe. Ah was haunted by ah ghoulish recurring nightmare where ahn enormous mutilated soldier was eating me from ma feet up and ah couldn'ae move, just wait to be devoured. I swear ah could feel every bit o' pain as ah was being greedily consumed.

Gradually the nightmares began to subside; no completely mind; ah don't think that'll ever come to be, but just enough to signal a change. After months and months o' nothing to do but ruminate oan ma daft choices, Elizabeth suggested that ah talk to ah new boy that'd come in; just as she had talked to me when ah arrived at the hospital.

'Ah'll be no use ta him,' ah protested. 'A useless cripple tellin' another that things aren't so bad? Thasall he needs.'

'It may help you Campbell,' she said. 'Come oan.'

So, she wheels me down there to where he was sat on a bed. The centre of his face was wrapped in white bandages. Poor bugger had lost his sight after a bullet grazed across the front o' his face; took most o' his nose too. Elizabeth introduced me and walked away. To begin with ah couldn'ae speak, jus' study his helpless demeanour. A child-like whimper was emanating from him, then ah realised he was tryin' te cry. Cryin' yet he had no eyes to shed tears from; it was too odd to grasp. Ah suddenly felt like the one who was well-off. Slowly, over the weeks, ah started to get through to him and he opened up to me.

'Ah cannae see, Campbell. They took ma eyes.'

'Ah know, laddie. They took ma legs.'

'Guess we're both fucked, then,' he says. His mouth twitched as though it was tryin' to remember how to smile.

He told me what his hopes and dreams were before he was blinded. Ah told him o' mine too and how ma football career was going to be on hold for a little while. Ah did this more and more with other wounded soldiers, helping them to make sense o' their new world as ah made sense o' mine. To my surprise ah started to find a strange sense o' peace and belonging. Ah'd never really listened to anyone before; you know, really listened; not just to the words but what lay behind the words. Ah suddenly felt useful in a way ah never pictured ah could be. Through the conversations ah discovered what ah'd suspected; boys in the war could only be understood by boys in the war. Friends and family would visit but nothing would be said aboot the fighting or the injuries; like they hadn'ae even occurred. Ah'd hear mothers and fathers bangin' oan about Mrs Johnson's cat and trivial noansense like that while boys, limbless and crippled, would stare off into space hearing imaginary shells bursting in their heads. I don't blame them for trying to sustain a sense of normality; the men fightin' at the front have an impossible time rationalising the insanity of it all, never mind the folks back home, who said goodbye to their fit and healthiest, only to have them returned broken and reduced te nothin'. The human mind wasn'ae designed to comprehend any o' this dreadfulness; it hasn'ae the capacity.

Through ma counselling I found a connection with human beings that ah never envisaged, and, in turn, I slowly came out o' ma black slump. Ah knew ah had to move oan or check out; ah'm no quitter as anyone who knows me will tell ya.

Ah began to notice the world again; ma new world; different than before, on account o' the fact ah cannae experience it in the same way. Little things started to catch ma attention like the chatter o' birds, the scent o' flowers, the touch o' the wind and the sound o' leaves skittering on the paths. The sky is beautiful, I realised, like a forever changing work o' art. Ah began to paint it; cirrus clouds, billowy nimbus clouds and peach and crimson sunsets. Ah don't know how ah was never aware o' this stuff before. Maybe ah was jus' switched off o' summint. Maybe ah jus' took it all for granted.

I don't hold a grudge against Meg and Lewis; they're better off together. They're from the old world where the Campbell they knew and loved died. This Campbell doesn'ae fit into the reality they reside in. He's dead for alla us noo, poor boy. It was no easy for any of us.

Campbell the boy no longer exists. Ah'm now Campbell the man; broken and in constant pain, yes, but also somehow stronger and more complete. My eyes and heart feel fully open for the first time. Ah never thought it would take something so severe to make me see what it's all about; no flash, no dazzle, no screaming jilts. It's about love, understanding, helping yeh fellow man and making the best o' what yeh got. Don't get me wrong, ah have no wish to be like this but ah ahm, and that's that.

'Do ye want to go outside today?' Elizabeth says. 'Looks like it's going to be nice.'

The sunlight is flooding into the room and illuminating her. She rubs her eyes and smiles. That smile. Ah owe ma life and ma sanity to her; beautiful Elizabeth. She pushed me and gave me a purpose when aw ah wanted to do was die. She sees me; no my injuries. It goes beyond physical attraction; it's a meeting o' souls. We're to be married in three weeks.

Ma foot still itches so bad, but ah'm alive and that's no small thing.

'Aye pet, let's go outside.'

Ma diary goes into a drawer and ah close it.

# DEREK AND HIS CLOWN

## *Fee Simpson*

There was nothing amusing about Derek. Derek was a serious man, with a serious disposition and oft' furrowed brow. He had never really had the opportunity for joking in his long and serious life; he had never created opportunities for joking. He had moved to London at 14, travelling alone he arrived and moved in with an aunt he'd never met before. His aunt was a fierce woman and not one for laughter.

It was odd then that one January morning, whilst walking down the Southbank on his way to working as a cleaner at the Tate Modern (a gallery he mostly disapproved of) he fell in love with a clown. He had seen singers and violinists, even the occasional dancer, but never a clown performing beside the Thames. The clown contorted its body ridiculously and grotesquely. The clown's heavily made-up eyes were intense and focused. It looked to Derek as if the clown was glowing from inside.

The clown's jawline was strong and masculine but, though it was hard to tell, it looked as if the skin under the makeup was smooth, not stubbly. The clown had slicked back hair, an oversized prosthetic nose and wore a large tweed jacket. Scanning further down the body you could see distinctly that the clown had enormous breasts. Derek hoped the breasts weren't some jovial part of the costume. He had never thought of himself as gay. He'd always imagined himself settling down with a lady. He assured himself the breasts were real. Derek, realising he was late for work, walked on without looking back.

Morning after morning, in the once empty spot he walked past on the way to work, he saw his beautiful clown. He thought about being with the clown, about holding her large breasts in his large hands. The relationship remained in his head. He stood at a respectable five meter distance. He started arriving later and later into work. No one minded. Derek however was disappointed in himself and so started getting the earlier tube. He had a good amount of time to watch his clown, and still be prompt.

After a month of watching her from a five meter distance the clown approached him.

'You watch me perform every day but you never laugh, why do you watch me if you don't want to laugh?'

Derek had imagined striking up a conversation with the clown plenty of times, but he hadn't been prepared for such a direct question. Of course he had imagined himself talking to the clown. He'd imagined suggestive flirtation and trying to conceal his many and varied flaws. He hadn't planned for a conversation based on honesty. After a moment's thought he answered,

'Perhaps I am not a laugh out loud man, but you move something in me and I enjoy it.'

The clowns eyes narrowed at the suggested double entendre of 'move something in me,' but Derek had said it sincerely. The clown answered,

'If you enjoy it so much, I can be hired for a private show.'

And so it was that Derek hired the clown three days a week between 7pm and 8pm, which was as often as his budget allowed, if he'd been a rich man he'd have had her every day. The clown felt slightly awkward the first couple of times she went to his flat, he wasn't a very responsive audience member. He always paid and seemed grateful after, so she kept going. She would usually practice in front of her mirror of an evening. When she was with Derek she had to use his expressions as her reflection, looking for any slight movement in the eye or the hint of a smile. Over time she was able to read him perfectly and her routine improved.

Derek saw this improvement and loved the grotesque, physical way she reacted to each blink, each outward breath, each vague gesture he made. He wanted to make love to her, but he didn't want to scare her. There were boundaries. She was an entertainer, he was the audience. This was his house, she was his visitor. She was vulnerable on both counts. He did not want that vulnerability to make her uncomfortable. He saw the light in her he'd seen that first day. But she was a performer and it was impossible to tell if she lit up for him or for the sake of her performance.

In truth it was both. She grew to love the time she spent in his little flat, her stage, his carpet, barely big enough to contain her bolder gestures. She never interacted directly with him, when she performed in the street sometimes she would grab an unsuspecting member of the public and engage them in a ridiculous semblance of a waltz. She felt unable to do that with Derek. She kept her distance.

One day on his way to work Derek noticed her, his clown, setting up her pitch. He was about to raise his hand to wave at her when he saw him. He was the long haired musician who sang out of tune and usually preformed further down from the clown. The musician kissed the clown. Derek froze, he wanted to punch the musician in the face, throw him into the Thames. Derek kept his head down and walked quickly to work.

The next time she came to his flat he could hardly lift his head to watch her. She felt it, the cool disappointment in the air. Assuming it was her performance she grew insecure until finally, half way through trying to tame an invisible dog she stopped.

'What's the problem?'

She sounded annoyed. Derek didn't know what to say.

'Perhaps I should go?'

'No.' If she left now, she wouldn't come back. He knew that much. If only he could force himself to say something more.

'You can't make me stay and perform for you, you're not even watching properly.'

And then she saw him. His sad, serious eyes.

'Tell me.' She said.

Derek began to gesticulate crudely, a serious man saw a beautiful lady with enormous breasts and a pretend nose. His heart was pounding, he tried to tell her he loved her but she scared him. She was so brave and he was so shy. But they made friends and she became more beautiful before him. And then there was a musician, an evil, talentless musician who took her and kissed her and the serious man's heart cracked in his chest. He threw it away and could no longer lift his head to look at his beautiful clown.

She watched his performance, his thrusts and uncontrolled movements. She smiled, understanding perfectly. She picked up his cracked heart and pressed it back into his chest. Moving her hands round his chest she pressed into his back and drew him to her. She looked up into his eyes, dark and wide. She kissed him gently on his pursed lips. Feeling the prosthetic nose brush against his cheek he began to laugh. The laughter grew in his belly and thundered out of his mouth. She let him laugh, but kept holding him to her. He looked back into her made up face, he gently removed the oversized nose and kissed her.

The musician was gone, grateful to have something he could write a song about. And they had each other. The clown and Derek.

# ON THE ORIGIN OF THE SPECIES

*Rebecca Swirsky*


Pattie Heller watches Mara Anderson with the concentration of an astronomer, observing in the long-dead stars not her future, but her disappearing past. Pattie watches, and she mourns.

It was on a mild, comfortable Sunday afternoon that the Andersons' took possession of Will and Helen Ferris's 1930's five-bedroom property, the cul-de-sac's last. From her bedroom window, Pattie witnessed a life compartmentalised, shifted from vehicle to building in the form of pots and pans, wardrobes and hat-stands. Clearly, a home was being claimed, despite those victors not yet feeling at home. Three children trailed an abercrombie-and-fitch wearing husband, yet it was the wife who kept Pattie pressed against her window pane. From the flip-flops to the unstyled hair sprouting from its top-knot, to the laughter pealing from a crooked, over-large mouth, every detail was studied. Pattie saw it all and felt a change in the atmosphere, the humid, cooked quality before a thunderstorm.

The following morning, Mara Anderson played rounders with the cul-de-sac children, including Pattie's two young sons. Pattie fingered her son's blue inhaler and heard the *thwack* of a ball being roundly, contentedly hit. Sliding a leg of lamb into the oven, Pattie saw Mara again leaping for the ball, tanned arms spread wide, sharp cries of 'I'm here!' hovering in the hazy air.

After supper, Carissa from number twenty-two stopped by. Mara's husband had joined her husband's accounting firm. And Mara, she added, had worked for the Natural History Museum, 'before'. Carissa's nose wrinkled as she presented Pattie with a holiday gift.

'Didn't you work there, Pats?'

'Once,' agreed Pattie vaguely. 'Super oil.' And she held the palm-sized gift of olive oil, fussy in tinted cellophane. It was a kind easily found in any major supermarket.

After Pattie's two sons were settled with homework, Pattie typed Mara's name into Google. Dr Mara Anderson's old department of Palaeontology staff page appeared. In the accompanying snapshot, Mara's shirt collar was undone. Her shoulder-length yellow hair was crinkled as if damp. Her gaze was steady, as though deciphering the horizon. Mara looked, Pattie decided, like many of the researchers and staff members at the Natural History Museum. She looked as Pattie had recalled herself looking. When Pattie's husband Sol strode down the hallway, sound of the toilet flushing, Pattie turned still.

At dinner, Pattie observed her family. Sol had replaced his grey work suit with pressed jeans and polo shirt. He actively enjoyed exchanging one uniform for another, a habit Pattie had for many years assumed ironic. Two decades earlier, Pattie's undergraduate degree in Archaeology and Prehistory had been swiftly followed by a PhD in Zoology. She'd looked to the future by investigating the past. Then, after two young babies and Sol's career in construction law, life's momentum had swerved to the aggressive demands of the present. To the *now*. Gazing at her sons' freshly washed hair gleaming with summer light, their heads down in a rare moment of silence, Pattie wanted to stroke those heads – hard. Cal was an arrival Pattie puzzled over, since precautions had been taken. She'd previously wondered whether her sons had consulted with each other pre-birth, hatching a plan in the corridors of her fallopian tubes in order that they might follow each other with breathtaking speed.

'Ma?'

Trent, Pattie's oldest at seven, stared. Pattie's friends and neighbours regularly commented on Trent's delicate, lightly-drawn features. He suffered life-threatening asthma – partnered by an immune system including more allergies yearly. Pattie is used to being hyper-alert when Trent stays with friends. She's activated the epi-pen more times than she can remember. She carries Piriton like some Americans shoulder guns. Some nights she lies awake, wondering whether Trent's allergic reactions will include her.

Cal's features are cast with impatience, their modelling squarer, plainer. Pattie and Sol had been initially uncertain – could their child really have ADHD? Now Pattie's a specialist at understanding Cal's thought processes. She's an expert at sliding underneath and around his mental pathways. *'Ma-listen-listen-ma-listen-listen,'* is what she hears, a daily necklace hung around her neck.

'Pattie?' Sol, a comfortable man, now frowns, knife gripped in his hand like a spear.

In the metallic silence that followed, Pattie ticked off her gifts. The boys. Sol's awareness of their different needs. Her health. Still, despite the chairs being evenly spaced around the table's four corners, there was the sense her husband and sons were facing her in a firing line. Her thoughts drifted towards the cold storage warehouses in South Kensington, the vast, curated stillness of those long-dead mammals.

'How's your biology project, Trent,' she asked, finally.

Trent blinked precisely, three times. 'Miss Smythe said if I got the African snails, it was more than enough.'

Trent's speech was clipped. He liked things neat. He demanded the world be presented in bite-sized portions.

*More than enough.* Pattie nodded and began stacking plates.

Monday morning, Pattie watched Mara dismantle what had been Helen Ferris's rockery. With each rock removed, Pattie sensed an internal dislodging, her ears clicking like pressure shifting. On impulse, Pattie signed up for a ceramics taster class at The Pottery Barn. The Barn was near her son's school, a place Pattie was called for allergic or behavioural emergencies. She regularly drove Cal down country roads, past windfarms and rapeseed fields, Simon & Garfunkel playing softly on the stereo. Her tank was kept full for that purpose.

Stepping into a lofty outhouse, Pattie removed her wedding ring. She ducked her head into a stiff, clay-smeared apron. Two hours later, a rust-coloured looseness rolling in waves, a cheque was written for the course. A pattern began, as though it had always been there. Mondays, between 10am and 12pm, Pattie occupied red-stained time. Epi-pens, inhalers, clocked-up drives and schedules floated away. Pattie was praised for the purity of her focus. With a smack in her heart, Pattie realised she'd begun those classes for Mara. Pattie couldn't say why, but the tall, boneless Giacommeti-style vases and shallow dips of stretched bowls contained Mara's essence. Mara, she knew, was a single, stilled heartbeat, contained in the porous clay.

Pattie made biscotti. She used good quality ingredients. While Cal was logged onto a computer war game, and Trent at a friend's house, Pattie knocked on the Anderson's front door. Mara's weighted gaze slid over Pattie's dove-grey pearl earrings, cream silk cardigan and pressed navy jeans. *I need all that you see,* Pattie silently replied.

Aloud, she said, 'I brought biscotti.'

'Wow, so thoughtful, thanks.' Mara pushed at fraying curls with the back of her hand. 'Come in while I sort the kids uniforms?' Pattie stared. Navy mascara had smudged into Mara's laughter lines. The bottom two buttons of her crumpled shirt were undone, exposing stretch-marked skin. Her hips were small and neatly wrought, like a boy.

Pattie did not come in.

Over the coming weeks, Pattie took nourishment from her bedroom's vantage point. The cul-de-sac's steep angle enabled her to observe the Anderson family picnicking in the garden, their sprawling limbs appearing to halt the dimming light. When the odd plastic cup and napkin was left, Pattie resisted the urge to climb through the garden hedges and hoard these items for safe-keeping, order and label them as though exhibits.

Wednesday morning, nosing her Subaru into the driveway after a Pottery Barn class, Pattie saw Mara framed by her top-floor window, speaking into her mobile. After that, Mara was often seen staring blankly as she ushered her children into the car or picnicked with her family. To Pattie, Mara seemed a person transfixed by the glowing tipping point of her days.

Yet when Pattie opened her door to find Mara holding a modest white package, she saw once again Will and Helen Ferris's rockery. As though in reverse, she saw each rock settling into the indented hollow previously left in the soil. Pattie's package, said Mara, contained flap-jacks. On a cardboard label, Pattie's own name was written in royal-blue calligraphy.

Pattie paused. 'You needn't have gone to such effort.'

There was a slight pause. 'Oh, I should,' said Mara, frowning.

Pattie learnt all the cul-de-sac had received flapjacks. People were relieved Mara was 'settling in'. As though Mara had been dragging her feet, had in some way they could not quite articulate, been holding back.

Although they'd worked in different areas, they'd poured years of study into their respective fields. Severing an identity would always be painful. Pattie's own area of expertise had been the mammals, a species over time supple and fluid in adaptation. Cal and Trent had taken it for granted they rode expensive bikes in streets that were wide and safe. During the holidays, their whooping catcalls silvered the dusk. Still, Pattie's dreams began to be inhabited by *their* museum, hers and Maras. Nightly in sleep, Pattie visited the museum's labyrinthine warren, its nave-like nooks in which staff had offices. She re-familiarized herself with the museum's devout-looking jumble of spires and towers connected by gothic Romanesque windows, so like a grand cathedral.

Pattie's living-room is loud with the splashy, showy absence of people having moments-ago left, and her coffee table is strewn with muesli bar wrappers. Pattie and Mara face each other. Their husbands, smelling lightly of sweat and summer ease, have driven the children to the bowling alley.

'God,' says Mara after a pause. 'It's blood- I mean, very quiet.'

'Yes,' agrees Pattie. Involuntarily she strokes her t-shirt. It is brushed-down ironed organic cotton. On the breast pocket is stitched the DNA's double helix ladder in shimmering blue thread. The shirt was Pattie's leaving gift from the Museum. The beauty of the helix, its compressed, curved code, never failed to take her breath away.

Now, if Pattie feels no anxiety, it's because she's planned each stage. When it's over, she'll call Mara's husband. She'll request Mara be left to rest. Perhaps she'll suggest a DVD for the children. Like anything, like history, fact and fiction will be blended. In the aftermath, it will be difficult to separate the two.

In the kitchen, the cafitiere is prepared. The smell is heady, despite being de-caffeinated. Pattie considers the pill. Its whiteness is placed against her dark-granite counter-top. A teaspoon is turned face-side down on a saucer. Coffee is poured. The pill slipped in. Each action has been so rehearsed it's become ritualised, part of a process.

Handing Mara her coffee in the living-room, Pattie notes Mara's earrings. A silver-pink pearl hangs in Mara's left lobe.

A much lighter, moon-yellow orb blooms in the left. Mara is wearing pearls, but they are mismatched pearls.

Mara's eldest is discussed. Moving homes has made him restless. He misses London, his old life. When Pattie asks, 'your specialism was in Palaeontology?' she flinches at a sound beginning and ending on the wrong notes for happiness.

Mara's laughter dies. 'Was. Couldn't keep travelling to get the data I required. Tom wasn't too bad, but after Lianna and Ed, no it had to stop. Some of my best fossil work was in the desert.' Mara tilts her head to speak to the past. 'Those dry, humid environments. Montana, South Dakota, Wyoming. And museums. Wonderful field trips to China and Canada. Switzerland.' Mara looks at Pattie lazily. 'It's the constant proving yourself in academic journals, the outputting. Yet I so miss cycling to my desk in under fifteen minutes from Kings Cross.'

'You'll adapt,' says Pattie neutrally.

Mara blinks, sits upright among aggressively-stuffed cushions, then falls back.

'Being with like-minded people was great, you know? Then I'd return to my empty hotel room and think of my children. They were too young. I couldn't make the two... halves of my life fit. Yes, we came here for a better life.' Mara is delicately slurring.

'Will you work, do you think?'

'Volunteer, maybe.' Mara's left eye is drooping. 'Whatever I can do around the kids schedules. Geology I've liked. But even with skeleton staff and volunteers there's hardly any funding.' A sigh escapes. Mara slumps, then surrenders. Pattie breathes out. Mara is now still as any of the mammalian specimens Pattie has catalogued. A museum is a place where visitors may examine evidence. Pattie recalls the vaulted, stunned silence filling the museum's South London warehouse. Each of the Asian, dwarf and water buffalo varieties had been posed differently, tagged with unique reference numbers given by Pattie. The possibilities of the future present through the past.

Pattie laces fingers with Mara in a slack grip. She is curating for future preservation what Mara is losing. Closing her eyes, her own tears are a shock – yet their presence is not shocking. Her tears are for days that spring open at 6am and snap shut at 10pm. For being unable to halt what she began eight years ago with the person she loved. For gaining so much, and it not being enough. For the varieties and subdivisions of perfection that exist.

At Pattie's party, the Zoology management team had gathered close. *Our lives are collections curated through memory,* the director had said theatrically. In the low light of the room used for goodbyes, sober faces had nodded. Then the director had clapped his hands and changed the mood by telling a joke, a queasy word-play between geckos and stereo players. Yet, thinks Pattie, as she props Mara among cushions damp with saline tide-marks. The similarity between curate and create is no coincidence.

On the hallway phone, Mara's husband tells her that *Toy Story 4* is playing. What Pattie hears is that her husband is enjoying a second whisky nightcap. Back in the living room, she finds that Mara's scarf has slipped to the floor, its blue cloth kinks ripples on water. Folding the scarf neatly and tucking it in her pocket, Pattie listens to their breathing, waves on a beach, never quite in sync. When she is ready, she holds her most elegantly stretched clay vase above her head.

Decades on, braided with the regular hiss of the morphine machine so that it seems both a present-day recollection and part of a further past, Pattie will relive this memory. As her husband and grown-up sons press close, their expressions hungry and urgent, Pattie will see once more the shattered vase, its component pieces, the base, the body, the tilted lip, all leaking red dust. She will relive presenting Mara with a thin, nearly translucent sheet of paper, and the peculiarity of Mara's expression as she gazed at the handwritten biscotti recipe in her lap, written in royal-blue calligraphy.

# SOMEBODY ELSE'S LIE

*Barney Walsh*

Most mornings, Mike has breakfast in a greasy spoon round the corner from his flat. It's not the most health-giving of places, forever about to be shut down, but it's more home than his tiny kitchen. He's come here for years. They know his name – or they might do one day, he reckons. One day they might say *Morning, Mike* when he steps in the door, as if he belonged. Till then, he does get a nod of recognition, sometimes. He has the full English breakfast, always: eggs, bacon, sausage, mushrooms, fried tomato, fried bread, beans; about as much as they can cram on the plate, basically. It all gleams with fat; you can feel your cholesterol rising just looking at it. A mug of tea to slosh it all down with; spots of fat floating on the surface of that, too.

But come one morning, Mike pushes open the door and there's a new girl behind the counter. Late teens, pretty. Her hair tied back in short tight bunches. When she takes his order – 'For you, please?' – and her accent comes out foreign, his disappointment lasts only a moment.

'Full English fry-up and a large tea, please, love.'

'Okey-doke.'

He folds his paper to the crossword, but he's rubbish at it today for some reason. Her accent something Eastern European, Polish or Romanian or one of those, they're all the same to him. It's too late for him to start learning names of countries. Doesn't matter, she's here now – one of us. He's fine with that. It surprises him that he's fine with it: none of the other lads he works with have nice things to say about your odd or unusual accents, or skin colours. Mike worries he's a bit strange, but honestly, he's not bothered that his full English is served by someone who's not.

She puts his plate down before him, points of light glittering on the fat.

'Ta, love. New here, aren't you? What's your name?'

'I'm Janina.'

'Well, good luck to you, Janina,' he says, reaching for the ketchup.

She smiles briefly and goes back to other people's breakfasts.

Now why'd he say that? Sounded like he was sending her off, like she were leaving already. He's an idiot. You should never try and talk. At least he'd not Englishified her name to Janine, she must get that a lot.

He starts on his breakfast, pretending to look at the paper; he slices egg, bacon, sausage, spears it all on his fork and digs it into the beans. Gobful of that: lovely. Sidelong, he watches the girl crack eggs, butter bread, sizzle sausages. Fried-egg sandwiches that squirt yolk when you bite them. Long, slender brown limbs. If he were ten years younger... Twenty years, more like. And he's not. She brushes loose strands of hair from her face with the back of a hand: lovely. Shit, he's fallen in love. Not even finished his breakfast. But who wouldn't love a girl who can do you a fry-up like this?

By the end of the week he can just say *the usual* and she knows what that is. Not that it's complicated, but it's more than the girl before her could manage in years. Janina keeps the place cleaner, too: the tables not so sticky, the frying pans and bubbling pots all shinier somehow. Keep at it like this and the place's hygiene rating will be up to something better than Barely Adequate.

Day after day, he barely speaks a word to her. What could he say, what'd be the point? There's nothing interesting in his life, his job. She's not bothered about scaffolding and concrete. It's all empty. You have to be not empty, if you want to imagine a woman might talk to you. And he's too old for her, he does know that: old enough to be her father. A young father, but still. Plus big fry-ups every morning and umpteen pints of an evening haven't given him a figure many women could fall for, certainly not a pretty young girl like Janina.

Anyway, he's not really in love, not properly. It's just a thing in his head, that's all. It's, like, a dream of a ghost of a memory of love. Shit, he should've been a poet. He fills the words into his morning crossword, ignoring the clues, slotting them in wherever they'll go. It's not that he's in love, it's not. It's more like, seeing her every day, he can sort of imagine how it might happen, how he could fall in love with her if he'd let himself. He can pretend how it might be possible. Or how *anyone* could fall in love with her, doesn't have to be him. And that's enough. Though he can't help thinking: if he'd felt even this much for his wife, what might that marriage not've been capable of?

Weekends, he has the same breakfast but goes to a bar in town instead, where he can wash his full English down with bitter, not tea. A couple pints of a morning. In the afternoon he goes home and does nothing, naps a bit, watches the racing or whatever on TV, till it's time to head to the pub for the evening. But one Sunday afternoon, the phone rings. He's sure it's one of those cold-calling sales bastards, almost tells them to get stuffed even before they've said anything, but then good thing he didn't, 'cause it's his ex-wife. It's been what, three years? Four?

'I'm just calling to see,' she says.

'To see what?'

'To see about you.'

'What, d'you miss me?'

'Don't be stupid. *God*, no. Happiest day of my life, finally being rid of you. But it's like, I can't help wondering. What're you up to. How saggy has your face got. How shit has your life turned without me. Stuff like that.'

'It's no worse without you,' Mike says. 'No worse, no better.'

'You're a liar. Anyway but also, I'm getting married again.'

'What? Oh shit. I mean, congratulations. Or is it congratulations I mean?'

'He's not at all like you.'

'Well that'll be nice for you. May your new life be a lot less awful than your old one.'

'Thanks. I'd say you too, but we both know it's not going to happen.'

This goes on for a few more minutes. He stops listening when she starts describing her fiancé. He's in management, his divorce'll be through soon. He'd rented a limo to propose to her, stuffed it with flowers. Mike stops listening. As soon as she hangs up, he heads for the pub, early as it is. He needs to be not alone. Those pints with his breakfast not enough. His ex-wife always makes him feel like this. Alone. Even when they were living together.

But on the way to the pub he passes the cafe and is surprised to see it's open on a Sunday. The place is empty; Janina's alone, sweeping the floor. How many shifts does she do of a week?

'Oh, hello,' she says, as he pushes open the door. 'You have come at the wrong time for your full English. Either you are way too late, or you are way too early.'

'Just a tea, please, Janina.'

He takes his usual table by the window, from where he can look out the window and watch the world passing by, or survey the cafe's insides, see what's what and who's who. There's no other customers this afternoon, and not much of a world outside either, not on a Sunday. He watches Janine. She plops teabag into mug, adds hot water from the tank, splashes in milk. Brings it over.

'Ta, love.'

Say something else? Like what? But she's doing it for him, lingering by the table, inspecting her trainers and not going away.

'You are troubled,' she says. 'I can tell.'

He spoons in his three sugars.

She backhands a lock of hair from her cheek; it falls straight back into place, like always. 'You are having a bad day.'

It does something to him, the surprise of this: there's someone in the world, after all, who can tell when something's wrong, someone who's willing to at least pretend she gives a shit. He has to put his spoon down. Just when you think there's no more wonder in the world.

'Just heard from my ex-wife,' he says.

'Is she wanting money?'

'No, she's always had more than me. She's getting married again, to someone who's not me. She's like you, I guess. Wants a new life.'

'Like me?'

'Yeah, y'know, coming here. A new start. That's what my ex-wife's after.'

'She can't have one,' Janina says, shaking her head as if delivering judgement.

'No?'

'No. No one can get you a new life. You can't run away from yourself.'

'Is that what you tried to do, to run away from yourself?'

'I am running away from other people.'

'Oh. Right.' He doesn't know what to do with this conversation. But they're talking, they're *talking* – keep it going. He tries, 'Well new life or no, I hope she'll be fucking happy. Oh, sorry – pardon my Greek.'

She laughs. 'I am not Greek,' she says, misunderstanding him. He's not sure he's ever seen her laugh before. But then laughs can't come easy, working in a dump like this. At last he's seeing it. You step in the door and this fine, invisible mist of animal fat settles on your skin: no place for a girl like her.

'Did you have children, your wife and you?'

'My ex-wife. My extremely *ex*, ex-wife. No, no kids. Thank fuck for small mercies, forgive my… uh, Russian?'

'Guess again.'

'Kids, no – not for me. Now you no doubt, one day—'

'I have a little boy.'

'Bit young for that, aren't you?' he says, annoyed with himself even as the words come out – doesn't want to be judgemental. 'You're what, seventeen?'

She smiles. 'I am twenty-three.'

'What's your son's name, then?'

'Wait,' she says. She goes behind the counter and into the back, returns a moment later with a photograph. She slides it across the table to Mike.

'In this, he is two. He is four, now.'

The photo can't have been taken locally – that's never English sunshine, it's too clean somehow. There's three of them in this sun: Janina, a man slightly older than her, a little boy. They're all perched on the edge of an old, crumbling stone fountain. Pure-white, foamy water plunges and splashes behind them. The man – nondescriptly good-looking – is the centre of the picture: the boy rides on his shoulders, pulling his ears; Janina leans in against him, her arm around his waist, her cheek pressed to his. The man's hand slides between her knees. They're all grinning: perfect, toothsome smiles that make Mike feel he's never seen a real smile till now.

Janina sits at the next table, draws her feet up onto the plastic chair, clasps her ankles in her hands. She rocks slightly, but watches him, eyeing his reactions. It's like a test, some kind of test.

'That the lad's father?'

'Yes. I would cut him from the picture, except it would cut my boy, too. I think maybe that is why he holds on to him like that, to lock himself to us, in the picture at least. So I couldn't slice him out later.'

'But he's…'

'He is gone. Or it is more like I am gone, my boy and me, we are gone – he is left behind. And that is best.'

'Okay. Still, it looks like a happy time.'

'It was not. It was a bad day. The picture is a lie.'

'So why keep it, then?'

'Because my boy is not a lie,' she says. She's not looking at Mike, she hugs her knees tightly to herself. 'It was a bad day, he hurt me very much. And it was another day, not long after that, when I saw in his face that soon he would be hurting my boy as he hurt me. Or worse. And so we stole ourselves from him.'

Mike looks at her, totally at a loss. She still doesn't raise her face. This is the test: this is him failing the test. What's she doing, sharing the pain? Does that halve it, or double it?

'He is a monster,' she says.

He looks at the picture again: it's just a lad, a normal young lad, happy young father with his gorgeous girlfriend and beautiful baby son. Blessed, envy-making.

She's never told anyone this before, he's sure of that. Even so little as what she's saying now. So why's she telling *him*, of all the nobodies who come in here? Because he's nobody. He didn't matter. A random stranger. She was telling it to the wind. But he thinks that in a moment he might find something to say – pull something *wise* for once from deep inside himself – to prove her wrong, show her he's not just no one… and then the cafe's door bangs open and men stomp in. Had to happen. Grumpy workmen having to work on a Sunday. Janina rises, slides herself languidly back behind the counter, takes their order, turns to fry bacon for their butties.

What's left of Mike's tea is cold. He stands, the photograph still in his hands.

'I'll say goodbye, then,' he says. The men glance over at him.

Janina, busy, doesn't turn. 'Okay,' she calls. 'Bye-bye, Mike.'

She knows his name. She'll always know it, now. For a while, anyway. He slips the photo into his coat pocket. He goes, but pauses with the door half-open. He doesn't know what's going on with his head.

'Shut the door, mate,' says one of the blokes. 'It's draughty.'

He goes to the pub. He props up the bar, as usual. There's a match on the TV, but only some obscure European teams – he doesn't follow footie close enough any more for it to mean anything. The pub is dark, and quiet. On his second or third pint he takes the photograph from his pocket, and looks at it. Can you put together a whole day, a whole life, from one stolen moment of it? Even though you know it's a lie. He thinks if anyone asks – the girl behind the bar, or one of the few other drinkers he knows by sight – if they ask, he can lie. He can say – what? This is my niece? My daughter? My girlfriend? No one'd believe that. He could say it was taken years ago: claim the lad in the photo is him when he was young. You wouldn't believe it now to look at me, but once I was young and fit. And the girl? Love of my life. She broke my heart, it never mended itself. Maybe he could make up a romantic lie like that. He's curious to find out what he will say, actually, if anyone asks about the photo. But no one does.

He knows he'll have to give it back. He's sure she'll ask for it back next time he's in. He'll say he took it accidentally, stuck it absent-mindedly in his pocket. He reckons he looks enough of an idiot you could believe he might do that by mistake. But Monday morning, when he's in for his breakfast, she doesn't ask. She just smiles and brings him his breakfast. They don't talk more than that. By the end of the week, she's still not asked for her picture back, he's still not offered it. She must've forgotten she'd shown it him; she must just think she's lost it. He leaves it too long to claim it was by mistake. He'll have to deny all knowledge, if she asks. But she never does. He tells himself it won't be her only copy, they're all digital nowadays, he's not taking anything she can't replace. He tells himself it doesn't matter, if he keeps it.

He never speaks to her again, not properly. Only to say *please* when he orders his breakfast, *thanks* when she puts his plate down before him. She always has a smile for him, and he notices that she doesn't have a smile for all her customers, not even most of them. But there's never any more than that. Till one day she's gone – it's not a job anyone would stay in long, not if they can help it – and a different woman serves him his breakfast: a fortyish blonde with an annoying laugh, as English as the breakfast. He doesn't even ask after Janina. The breakfasts get worse, in bits variously undercooked or burnt.

He carries the photo in his wallet, takes it out every now and then – most days, in fact. Maybe she deliberately let him steal it; maybe it's a gift. Probably not, but maybe. He looks at the girl, the young man, the child. He stares at the picture, tries to decode it as if it were a crossword clue. But he could never do the cryptic, he only does the quick one – and it's not quick when he does it. It's not that he's in love with her. He never was, he's sure of that now. He doesn't know what it is. It's not that he thinks of her as a daughter, either – he hasn't the right – or even that he wishes he'd had a family, like this perfect one in the photo. Because he knows the photo's a lie, she'd told him that herself. But it's a lie he likes being told, somehow. It's a lie he can play along with, if not believe in. If that makes sense. Whatever, he's glad to have it, this small piece of somebody else's life, somebody else's lie.